THE SONS OF ISHMAEL

George Berguño was born in Princeton, New Jersey, and raised in Virginia. Thereafter he lived and worked in several countries including Chile, France, Austria, and Russia. He began studying psychology at the American University in Paris, and completed his studies at the University of London. His short stories have been published in the USA and the UK, and featured in several anthologies, published most notably by Ex Occidente Press and Egaeus Press. He now resides in London, where he teaches psychology at an American university. He is the author of four collections of short stories, the first of which was *The Sons of Ishmael*.

GEORGE BERGUÑO

THE SONS OF ISHMAEL

For my grandfather,

Jorge Berguño Meneses

1893-1983

CONTENTS

INTRODUCTION

THERE is a short story by the Mexican writer Juan José Arreola in which a young man, who is troubled by the evil in the world, writes a letter to God. The letter arrives in the 'galleries of silence' and God takes a mild interest in the man's existential questionings; but God's response is limited to giving banal and useless advice. 'In your place,' God replies, 'I would look for a gardener's post or cultivate a garden patch of my own. With the flowers in it and the butterflies that would come to visit them, you would have enough to make your life happy.'

I discovered Arreola's story at a time in my life when I was grieving over the loss of a friend. When Adam* died in the autumn of 1998, murdered by an unknown passerby, I went through the typical expressions of grief: surprise, tears, the funeral, flowers, condolences and sleepless nights. I visited the site of the murder; I planted a tree in my garden and gave it his name; I talked to the police; I prayed. But the details of the murder continued to haunt me. I wanted to be-

---

* The name is fictitious, to protect the victim's family.

lieve that there was some technique I had overlooked: a method or healing procedure by which I could lay the haunting to rest.

Adam was twenty-seven when he decided to go fishing in London. It was a cool Saturday morning when he made his way to Regent's Canal in faded overalls and a brown felt cap. Selecting a quiet spot in which to cast his line, he sat and waited for the fish to bite. Shortly before ten o'clock, a stranger—a bearded man in a worn-out suit—approached the youth and asked, 'Can you spare some change?' Adam ignored the request, so the intruder repeated the question, and added, 'I'm thirsty.' But my young friend remained silent, his eyes fastened on the end of the fishing line. Suddenly, from out of the stranger's jacket came a knife, and the knife, wielded by a quivering hand, plunged into the young man's chest. Blood burst forth, and the victim's body, surprised by the sudden onslaught, shook violently and then lay still.

The stranger now searched the victim's pockets and in a side lining of the overalls he found some coins—not many, but enough to satisfy his immediate desire. The assassin pocketed the coins, marched away from the dead body and at the first public house he encountered, he ordered a glass of house wine which he paid for with the blood money. Some time later, he found himself staring in surprise at an empty glass and felt sad and angry that the drink had ended. He soared out of the public house and made his way back to the canal. There, he found the corpse, and, pointing an accusing finger at the dead man, he cried, 'Why didn't you carry more money? Didn't you know I was thirsty? I'm still thirsty!' And it was while he thus ranted and groaned that two police constables stumbled upon him. They questioned him about the body and escorted him to the nearest police station, where later that afternoon he confessed to murder.

The story I have just reported is a true account, told in its bare essentials and unadorned by fictional elements. When news of Adam's death reached me, I marvelled at the absurd economics of existence: for a glass of wine a life had been snuffed out. But to understand the full extent of my grief, I must now reveal to the reader that for two years prior to his death Adam had been in treatment. I need not disclose what compelled him to seek psychological help; it will suffice if I say that he was in great pain. Over the two years of treatment, he succeeded in using therapy to construct a personal narrative that allowed him to bear his pain. Indeed, at the time of his death he was ready to return to the everyday world of loving and working. But a stranger had come along and exchanged his life for a drink. Along with his life, the stranger had also exchanged the two years of intense psychological work that Adam had engaged in—with a swish of the knife his efforts had been obliterated.

In the years that followed, I became aware of the inadequate nature of advice when confronting the deepest matters of the heart. I received many comforting expressions of concern from friends, and not one item of advice reached into the core of my dilemma. The comforting professional tactics of priests and counsellors were equally futile. And I spent many years trying to find a solution to my psychological scar. In time I realised that my pain was metaphysical or—to use the language of our times—existential. It was this insight that permitted me to shift my attention away from the search for a solution and to concentrate my efforts on understanding the question.

'Why is good so defenceless?' writes the anonymous narrator in Arreola's story, 'Why does it crumble so easily? Scarcely a few hours of strength are carefully built up when a blow of a minute comes to topple over the whole structure. Every night I am overwhelmed by the ruins of a day destroyed, of a day that was beautiful and lovingly built.'

When I first read these lines I was struck by the echo of my own pain: I could have written those words. Indeed, I could have written the entire story. Of course, the reader might argue that the question that compelled Arreola to pen his story—why is good so defenceless?—was my very own. And the reader would be right. But what impresses me now is not the coincidence, but the way the question embedded in Arreola's story is directed to a world beyond our own. The tone of Arreola's narrator is the voice of despair; and it is this voice that characterizes the real story.

One day, I experienced a sense of liberation when I came across a fragment of a diary that Maxim Gorky had kept during his travels through Russia. The fragment was entitled 'A Strange Murderer' and consisted of a confession made by a judge shortly before his death by cancer of the stomach. In his narrative, the judge describes how over his long career only one murderer had ever awakened in him the 'feeling of terror of man before man.' The murderer in question was the packhorse-driver Merkuloff, a broad-shouldered man in his mid-forties with a face 'such as one usually sees on holy images.' What particularly impressed the judge was the murderer's expression of pity in his eyes and the manner in which he talked about his crimes without trying to justify himself or arouse compassion in his listener.

Merkuloff's first murder is committed one autumn while carrying a sack of sugar from the harbour. Suddenly, he notices that a man is walking behind his cart. The stranger has cut a gash in the sack and is filling his pockets with sugar. Merkuloff does not hesitate in taking the man's life by giving him a blow on the forehead. Nor does he hesitate in going to the police and confessing his crime. What is of special interest here is the tone of his confession. 'How is it, how can it be?' Merkuloff says to the judge, 'A man was walking along the road; I struck him—and—no more man. What does it mean?'

Because of the unpremeditated nature of his crime Merkuloff is given a mild sentence, and after his release from prison he is sent to a monastery to do penance. But he finds that the routines of monastic life do not alleviate his pain. One day, he addresses one of the monks, saying, 'I can kill you very gently, very softly—allow you to say a prayer first; then kill you. How do you explain that?' The priest's advice—that he should pray until he is exhausted—proves useless;

and Merkuloff continues to be terrified of the fragility of human life.

Gorky's portrait of the murderer is the story of a man who perpetuates evil while remaining terrified of his potential for cruelty. But Merkuloff's shame does not spare him from further crimes. On the contrary, his conscience drives him to commit more murders in a desperate search for an answer to his pain. Two years after his release from the monastery, he murders a young girl, and Merkuloff is sent to prison once again. Upon release he walks about in a daze, unable to understand anything around him, all the time reflecting on the fact that he could kill whoever he wants and that he in turn could be killed by a stranger at any time. He describes himself as 'a fly on a window-pane: the glass might break at any moment and I'd fall through, falling God knows where.' Finally, exhausted by his search for a solution to his dilemma, Merkuloff kills again and is returned to prison. He advises his jailors, 'You'd better tie up my soul—not my hands—you fools!' Days later, he strangles himself in his cell using the chains that he was manacled with.

Merkuloff's suicide is his ultimate response to the question of evil. To be precise, it represents the failure on the part of the law and organised religion to provide an answer to his existential plea. At first, I wondered why Merkuloff's confession to the judge—so clear and sincere—had not brought about a measure of healing. Then, I was reminded of my own failure to heal my pain. Why had I continued to grieve year after year? At last I had it: my story, like Merkuloff's, had not yet found the context in which it could be retold. In other words, healing does not dwell primarily in the telling of a story to a sympathetic listener, but in discovering that one's own story is a retelling of an ancient text.

Thus it was that by a long and convoluted path I was led to discover the limits of the law, religion and psychology. In their place I discovered the profound healing potential of literature. Juan José Arreola's anonymous narrator and Maxim Gorky's troubled murderer have been my companions in pain. They have served me as mentors in ways that teachers, priests and counsellors rarely achieve.

Since discovering Arreola's story, I have made many friends in the vast kingdom of literature. I have befriended men and women that I never met; men and women who died before I was born, but who left a record of their struggles with the imponderables of life. On many a sleepless night I have sat with Herodotus, or that shy and sensitive writer known as the Lady Sarashina. I have conversed with the anonymous narrator of that masterpiece of medieval literature, *Njal's Saga*. And I have found comfort in the writings of the spiritually homeless—Joseph Roth, Alexander Lernet-Holenia, Leo Perutz. It is to repay these—and many other—friends that I have written the stories to be found in *The Sons of Ishmael*, my first collection of short stories.

THE SONS OF
ISHMAEL

We were outfitted for life, only for death to greet us. We were still standing in bewilderment at our first funeral procession, and already we were lying in a mass grave. We knew more than the old people, we were the unhappy grandsons who put their grandfathers on their laps to tell them stories.

—Joseph Roth

NIGHT SEA JOURNEY TO TURKU

To the memory of William Heinesen

THE TAXI that swept onto the Stockholm pier on that warm damp evening in August was a shabby old thing. It rattled along and pulled up beside the Narvik—a ship bound for Turku. From the interior of the cab a youth emerged, bearing pale lips and anxious blue eyes. Shouldering a small bag with clean shirts, shaving implements, a packet of cigarettes and a book of Homer's verses, he boarded the ship. A moment later, the gangplank was removed, the foghorn gave its eerie blast and the ship left the pier.

The youth, who was a native of Copenhagen, had been wandering up the eastern coast of Sweden for three days—first by ferry, then by bus—for no other reason than to go as far north as possible before the summer ended. But upon arriving at Stockholm, he had decided that he would visit Finland. He told himself that he had always longed to see Helsinki and so the change of plan was entirely justified. The fact was that he had never given a thought to that mysterious country of lakes and forests; but he was a youth like any other, filled with the magic of self-deception.

Knowing that the crossing to Turku was an overnight trip, he approached the ship's steward—a broad-shouldered man with a neatly trimmed dark moustache—and requested a cabin for the night. The man with the dark moustache studied the youth carefully before replying, as if the request itself were an unusual event on this ship.

'You should have reserved a cabin,' the steward barked. 'This is the busy season. Most passengers will be sleeping in the lounge and restaurant tonight.'

The youth made his way down the labyrinthine corridors of the ship, climbing from deck to deck, but the steward's prediction had come true. The ship was surging with tourists, and it seemed the youth would never find a secluded corner in which to lay his head down for the night.

In the lounge, a jazz band was playing and couples moved to the shrill, plaintive tones of a saxophone. Repelled by the frantic contortions of the dancers, the youth made his way to the restaurant in search of a quiet table where he might sip some wine and let his thoughts meander. But no sooner had he entered the dining area than an unhappy incident took place. A fat man fisting a mug of beer collided with the youth, the beer spilling onto the youth's jacket. It was as if the restaurant itself were rejecting him, demanding that he be gone. The fat man apologized for his clumsiness. Holding the beer mug with one hand, he brushed down the youth's jacket with the other. But to the young man it seemed as if the coarse bloated hand that was trying to make things better was pummelling his chest.

He fled from the fat man; he ran away from the crowds, threading his way from room to room and staircase to staircase, until at length he reached the deserted upper deck, where he resigned himself to sleeping under the gentle shimmering of the arctic stars.

Sprawling his tired body onto a deckchair, he rummaged in his bag and found his cigarettes. He smoked lazily, and gazed out at the murky green waters of the Baltic Sea. In the distance: the faint lights of Stockholm—and the long arms of the setting sun glided on the waters, like a red and orange flower that refuses to wither.

All at once, he knew he was not alone.

A woman stood with her back to the sea, her fingers gripping the handrail. She was a tall woman of about forty, with weary eyes that seemed to peer out from deep in their sockets; only her long dark-brown hair stirred to the gentle caresses of the night breeze. She wore a long grey dress that reached down to her bare feet. A golden chain with a solitary pearl adorned her slim pale neck.

'May I?' she said.

The youth sat up.

Reaching into his bag, he brought forth the packet of cigarettes and offered it to her. But she remained standing, her eyes now riveted upon his face. Seeing that she made no effort to take the proffered cigarette, he withdrew his arm and remained sitting with the packet in his hand, silent and confused.

'Where are you going?' she asked.

He hesitated before answering, 'Helsinki.' Then, after a longer pause, 'I've always dreamed of going there.'

'I've always been making my way to Helsinki,' she said. 'But I've never been able to complete my journey.'

Then, as the youth pondered the woman's strange words, an extraordinary thing occurred. It was a moment of pure magic that he would remember time and again over the years, and recall on the day he died. The woman turned her head and looked down the length of the deck, revealing her magnificent profile. And as she did so, the sun gave one final desperate burst of light before it sank into the waters. The rays of the dying sun shone on the woman's hair, giving it a red tinge that transformed her. She became another woman, full of the splendours of youth; a woman of about eighteen years, eyes blazing with life, limbs poised for a dance.

The woman with the red-brown hair skipped gracefully to the deckchair next to the youth. She sat so close to him, he could smell her fragrance, see the brown of her eyes and hear her rapid, shallow breaths.

His throat parched, his hands trembled, his heart pounded.

'Aren't you afraid to be up here all alone, without anyone in the world to guide you?' she asked.

He looked down at his shaking hands, not daring to meet her gaze.

'I like to be alone,' he said at last.

'I'm always alone.'

They dug into silence like soldiers in their trenches. The Swedish flag crackled in the wind. The black velvet night shone brighter than the glaring white stars.

Suddenly, the woman rose and said, as if speaking to the wind, 'The hour is late. Where are you staying tonight?'

'I have nowhere to go,' he said mournfully. 'The cabins are all taken and I can't stand to be with the other passengers.'

'You'll catch cold if you stay here. Come with me.'

The woman's cabin was a cramped little box, with a narrow bunk and no electricity. Only the light from the stars at the other end of the universe, as it climbed through the porthole, allowed them to see their way in the dark. They lay naked, their bodies like parallel tracks, tense and burning for each other. She lay inert, encased in her mystery—like a jewel well set. At length the silent lovers were lulled to sleep by the gentle rocking of the waves and the distant clatter of the ship's engines. His sleep that night was deep; it reached into the very bowels of the earth.

When he woke next morning he found he was alone; the ship no longer rolled from side to side. He heard the shuffling of hurried feet and knew at once that the Narvik had set anchor. He dressed hastily, slung his bag over his shoulder and set about looking for his companion of the night. But the mad scramble to disembark had already begun and it seemed to the youth that every woman that he glanced at was the woman with the blazing red hair. He stared at the passengers, watched as they clawed their way down the gangplank, yelling and shoving, until only he remained. Was she still on board? Surely, she would not have left without exchanging farewells!

He descended into Turku, looked for her in the narrow lanes of the ancient port, sat in restaurants and coffeehouses, waiting. He wandered through the grounds of Turku Castle until the day grew bleak and tired. At dusk, he boarded the train to Helsinki, arriving a minute before midnight. For three days he searched for her in the dreary grey-stone avenues of the capital city. He waited by the harbour, took his meals standing in the Old Market Hall, prayed in the cathedral on Senate Square. By and by, he grew desperate and boarded the train to Joensuu. He searched for her by the lakes, roamed the forests by day, the lonely city streets by night; he forgot to sleep and journeyed ever northwards. In Oulu he boarded another train, bound for Norwegian Lapland. The sun grew cool as the train gained the Arctic Circle; the vast forests mocked him, the crystalline waters of the fjords witnessed his pain.

And then, the train broke down in a desolate spot. The guards marched into the compartments, informing the passengers that they would have to wait two days for a replacement train. But there was nothing to worry about, they said, food was plentiful and free, the weather was mild.

Preferring the silent evergreens to the company of his fellow passengers, the youth wandered into the nearby forest. Gathering dry spruce twigs and bark from the birch trees, he built a fire and for two days he sat by its flames and read Homer. He read that when

Odysseus and his sailors reached Circe's island, they came upon a stone house in the midst of a knotted forest, and were met by wolves and lions made meek by magic. From within the house there wafted the enchanting voice of the goddess of the island. Only Eurylochus, who was a kinsman of Odysseus, escaped Circe's charms and magic spells. As for the other sailors: they were transformed into swine. Alerted to the danger by Eurylochus and aided by Hermes, Odysseus subdued the goddess and forced her to be his lover. He remained on the island for months until his warriors—who had regained their human form—grew nostalgic for home. Circe knew she had to let Odysseus go, but she warned him that he would never gain home by sailing directly to Ithaca. To return home, he and his men would have to journey into the underworld, through the land of Death.

The youth reached the port of Narvik a month after his departure from Stockholm. Standing at the entrance to the northernmost railway station in the world, he knew the futility of further travel. That day, he sat on a lonely bench in the drizzling rain and watched as the boats bobbed up and down in the small harbour. At last, as the faint rays of the hidden sun sang their farewell, he lay himself down on a pebbled beach and wept.

He returned to his native Copenhagen, where he enrolled as a medical student at the university. The weeks flowed into months and the months soared into years. He graduated, became a general practitioner on the Gammeltorv Square, and his professional years saddened into decades. He loved one woman and then another, and each time, when his love was exhausted, he cast his mind back to the girl with the flaming red hair. Later, he married, divorced, remarried. His second wife gave birth to three children: two boys, one girl. He achieved all of his earthly ambitions and was recognised by his friends as a good father, a devoted husband and a competent medical man; his life became the model of a perfectly ordinary life, the kind of life that is not worth narrating.

In his sixty-fifth year he retired, and not long after he began to lose his memory. He forgot the past; he could not remember the highlights of his professional career; he forgot the name of his wife and the names of his children. In time, he forgot himself and did not notice when his wife died and his two sons deserted him. Only his daughter stood by him in his very old age and in the end, in his ninetieth year, even she abandoned him, leaving him in the care of nurses in a home for the elderly on the northeast coast of Denmark.

On the day he died, long thin arms of powdery sunlight crept into the long hall where the elderly residents gathered after breakfast, and where the more fortunate would be visited by a friend or a family member. The old man from Copenhagen sat in a wheelchair by a high window that looked onto the windswept beach, a blanket warming his lap. Vague sounds reached his ears: footsteps in the hall, a door opened and then shut, a chair scraped the wooden floors, soft voices fluttered about and—in the distance—the sad low tones of a solitary church bell.

A tall woman of about thirty-five had come into the hall with her daughter—a lively child with earth-brown hair and eyes like black moons. It was the girl's fourth birthday and the mother had brought her to see Grandma, a delicate white-haired woman who always sat alone in a corner. But the child was more interested in studying the expressions of the old folks than in anything that Grandma had to say. Suddenly, her eyes alighted on the old man from Copenhagen, and, led on by an irresistible curiosity she walked up to him with deliberate steps and said, 'What's your name?'

My name, he pondered, what is my name? But it had been many years since he could remember any-thing about himself.

'Do you live here?' the child continued.

He puzzled: is this my home? He looked about him, searching the withered faces of the old.

'Who are you?' she insisted. Her voice had risen ever so slightly.

The old man from Copenhagen turned his gaze upon the child. Something in her expression stirred the inner chamber of his being, releasing an image from the lost kingdom of his youth. He leaned for-ward and extended a wrinkled bony hand; but the girl stepped back and the image was gone.

'Mama!—Mama!' she cried.

The mother came running. Wrapping her arms around her daughter, she said, 'I'm here, darling, I'm here. I was just talking to Grandma.' Then, turning to the old man, she said in a hostile tone, 'I'm sorry if my daughter has troubled you.'

He watched while mother and daughter wandered away from him, hand in hand, and sat with Grandma for the rest of the morning. His eyes lingered on the child, searching that young face for a clue to the mystery of his existence, unaware that by evening he would breathe no more. Then, the women said their farewells: mother and daughter were departing. He watched them as they made their exit, realising at last that something was slipping through his grasp, that a fragment of his being was about to be lost. Then, at the last glance, as the girl and her mother pushed open the door to the outside world, a stray thread of sunlight fell on the girl's countenance, turning the brown of her hair into red flames.

In a dark corner of his soul, a rusty gate swung open, and his youth, long since buried in the land of the dead, came back to haunt him: the taxi on the Stockholm pier, Homer's verses in his bag, the immensity of the Baltic sky—and the beautiful stranger with the burning red hair, his silent companion on the night sea journey to Turku.

INTO THE ATACAMA 1899

Desert *apatheia* has a daughter whose name is love.
—Evagrius of Pontus

WHEN DOÑA TERESA died of a chronic sneezing condition that had lasted many years, Don Francisco, now a lonely man in his fifties, vowed to retire from the world.

Don Francisco buried Doña Teresa in *El Cementerio de las Almas Perdidas*. Then, after selling the old matrimonial home on Valparaiso Bay, and burning all that remained of his wife's possessions, he rode north on horseback until he reached the edge of the Atacama Desert—the loneliest and driest place on earth. There he found an abandoned mud dwelling with a straw roof and a fireplace made of grey stones. A well with fresh water was situated at twenty paces from the front of the house. He adopted these abandoned remnants as his new home.

Once a week, Don Francisco would ride twenty miles to the nearest village to buy provisions of dry meat and candles; as well as tobacco, gourds and beans—and red wines from Mendoza. He had been living at the edge of the desert for two years, when, one fine day, he rode into the village and came upon a fair. Long tables had been set up around the plaza and merchants were singing their wares. Don Francisco wandered about, looking here and perusing there, until he came upon a stall piled high with tattered children's toys. He stood gazing at the toys, his hands tucked into his thin leather jacket; his face basking in the fierce rays of the sun.

Suddenly, his left hand emerged from the comfort of his jacket and rummaged among the old toys. His hand crawled about, digging here and burrowing there, until his fingers came upon a tangle of black hair and the milky-white form of a naked young girl.

He rescued the girl-doll from among the broken toys and straightened her hair. She was a strange doll, made from material that he could not identify. Tiny strips of black silk were glued to her body, indicating that she had once worn a dress, as well as slippers. But now she was naked and one eye was missing, giving her a wasted look tinged with a streak of bitterness—as if the doll were mocking the hand that held her.

Don Francisco paid for the toy and strolled about town, the doll still clutched in his left palm. After a while, he sat on a bench and examined the old doll. At first, he had felt content with his new acquisition; two pesos had seemed a small amount of money to pay for an unusual toy. But now, looking at the doll with a critical eye, it struck him that the naked girl seemed ugly and grotesque, the helpless victim of the ravages of time. For an instant, he felt the compulsion to throw the doll into the dirt road. Instead, he thrust the doll into the left pocket of his jacket, retraced his steps back to the marketplace and bought his provisions for the week.

When Don Francisco returned home, he placed the doll over the fireplace and made ready for sleep. He poured water from a clay pitcher into a tin basin and washed the desert dust off his face. The sun had long since tired of travelling the sky, but there was no moon that night. He undressed, drank a glass of *agua ardiente*, turned out the lamp and slipped into bed. He fell at once into a deep and dreamless sleep.

Some time later, Don Francisco awoke. The darkness was absolute, but his instinct told him that a stranger was in the house. He reached for the revolver that he kept under the pillow and with cautious steps he made his way towards the front entrance of his austere dwelling.

A girl in a black dress was standing by the fireplace, her attention riveted upon the doll. Her long black hair was streaked with silver; her skin was of an uncanny whiteness. Her long thin fingers were grimy and her nails were torn; her lips were cherry-red. Don Francisco had never seen a woman of such intense beauty. But when the girl turned to face him, he witnessed her ugliness. There—where he had expected to find two young eyes—just above her delicate nose—he saw two cavernous hollows. And the impulse came upon him to flee; for he knew at once that she was not a living thing.

Slowly, very slowly, she walked past Don Francisco and into the moonless night.

The days ran on and the girl with the hollow eyes continued to visit Don Francisco. Day and night she glided soundlessly into the house and stared at the old doll. Although he fast became accustomed to her silent ritual, he tried to keep her out. But it was no use barring the windows and bolting the door: the girl would find her way in. She must be a desert-spirit, he thought; one of those spirits the villagers always tell about, who come in the night and drink the blood of chickens and cattle. Don Francisco feared for his horse. He had a rifle, but of what use could such a weapon be against a desert-spirit? He was alone, surrounded by a vast wasteland of sand and dust. There was no one to call on, no one to confide in. He would have to learn to live with the girl or persuade her to leave.

One day, he took the doll and placed it by the well. From that day on the girl no longer entered his house. She seemed content to gaze at the doll and showed no interest in Don Francisco or his house or horse. But her visits became more frequent. She came in the morning and hovered about all day. At night, he could hear her rustling about; he could feel her restlessness.

He tried to remember what his grandmother had taught him about the spirits. What did the spirits want? What magic could end their futile wanderings? But he had long forgotten the stories that his grandmother had recited to him as a boy.

And so, a day came when he made up his mind to talk to the girl.

It happened on a day when the sky turned orange and a wind from the west brought with it the smell of the sea. Shortly before nightfall Don Francisco returned with provisions. He unsaddled his horse and brought forth from his bag a freshly caught rabbit, eggplants and a bottle of red wine. He set about cooking the rabbit with strong herbs and frying the eggplants with lemon and breadcrumbs. He opened the wine and poured two glasses. When the rabbit was cooked tender and the eggplants were crisp, he set the food and wine on the table, lit a candle and went out to invite the girl.

Darkness was gathering and the first stars had settled on the Andes.

'Are you hungry?' he asked.

The girl turned about and studied his face. Then, with silent ponderous steps she walked past him and into his home. He followed her in and offered her a chair. He selected a portion of meat and eggplants and served them on a dish. He sat at the opposite end of the small table and pointed to the wine.

'Please,' he urged her, 'please begin.'

If truth were told, Don Francisco had not expected the girl to touch the food or drink the wine. He had never heard of a desert-spirit that would accept cooked meat. He watched in amazement as the girl gulped down the wine and devoured the food with her bare hands. Don Francisco set aside his knife and fork and he too used his hands to eat. And as they ate, he revealed the contours of his life.

His name, he told her, was Francisco Bretón, of the famous house of Bretón that descended from the first *conquistadores*. His family was an ancient one, more ancient than Spain itself and his family roots reached back to the Gaels who had fought against the Romans. But when he recounted the story of his unhappy marriage to Doña Teresa and the reasons that had brought him to the desert, he grew sad and words failed him.

Suddenly, the girl sprang to her feet and sang a beautiful-eerie song in a strange tongue. Don Francisco marvelled at the girl's voice: it reminded him of lost cities and autumn colours. A powerful mixture of nostalgia and joy took possession of his being. Though he could not understand the words, the song entranced him and pierced deep into his memories, bringing back lonely fragments of his youth.

A melancholic silence followed the girl's verses, a silence that Don Francisco would recall later as the solemn moment in which his old life ended and a new, terrible adventure began. Stirred to the depths by the girl's voice, he realised: although he had turned his back upon the world and embraced solitude as his permanent companion, he had not yet given up on life. And it was this girl—a desert-spirit—who had revealed his inner self to him.

'You sang beautifully,' he said at last, 'but I could not recognise the words.'

'That was an old story my mother used to sing to me when I was still a child and the world had not yet shown its cruel face. I sang in Quechua, my mother tongue.'

'So you are Inca!'

'I am one of the lost races, Don Francisco. My people once commanded a vast empire at the edge of a lake in the northeast Andes. When the *conquistadores* came on horseback, we mistook them for gods. Our foolishness cost us many lives, for these men—your people—murdered our men and enslaved our women. They burned our cities and mocked our gods.'

'Don Xavier Bretón, my ancestor…'

'…Was among the soldiers who burned and pillaged Cuzco.'

Don Francisco stared at the girl's lips; he could hear a moth fluttering; his throat had dried up.

'My name is Naira,' the girl said at length. 'My mother was Tamaya. My father, a tyrant whose name I shall not utter. I thank you for your kindness, Don Francisco. But now, I must depart.'

So saying, she walked out into the desert night.

Don Francisco remained in his chair for most of that night, wandering through the album of his youth. The girl's voice—where had he heard it before? Perhaps it had always been there: in his mother's commands, in the tall tales his grandmother had recited on sleepless nights, in the gentle stirrings of his first love, and yes, even in the bitter tones of Doña Teresa he had heard the future echoes of the girl's voice.

At sunrise, he stirred from his chair and plodded outside. He waited for the girl by the well, but for once she did not appear. His eyes roamed the horizon: they searched the land parched by the long whips of the merciless sun. At midday, he took refuge in the cool interior of his home, carrying the doll with him and placing it once again on the grey chimney. In the afternoon he fed his horse, but his heart was elsewhere. Where had she gone? Would she never return? She will come at sunset, he muttered to himself.

But the twilight shadows came, dragging an infinite silence behind them.

At last the girl arrived, carrying a bag filled with pieces of yucca, nuts, sweet potatoes and hearts of palm. Glancing at the ragged doll on the chimney, she said, 'I see she's back.'

Don Francisco smiled. 'I thought you'd gone forever.'

Naira gave a sudden laugh. 'Come—let's eat. I travelled far to find these poor morsels of food.'

Don Francisco brought forth another bottle of red wine and it seemed to him that he had never tasted a meal so fine. The girl nattered incessantly, and every now and then she would burst into contagious laughter. He listened in amazement to everything she said, and once again he heard her sing old tales of the Inca. Afterwards, she invited him to sing, but he made excuses, claiming a poor memory for songs. The fact was, Don Francisco's memory was a treasure house of literature, and he recited old poems by Cervantes and Garcia Lorca.

'Your *castellano antiguo* is most impressive, Don Francisco,' said Naira, laughing with delight. 'Anyone would think that you had lived hundreds of years ago.'

Indeed, Don Francisco had often felt as if he belonged to another century. His years in Valparaiso had been unhappy ones, not so much because of his sad marriage to Doña Teresa, but because he had never adapted to the codes and conventions of that immoral city. He had strived to lead his life along firm paths and clung to values of a long gone era. Doña Teresa, for her part, had breathed a different atmosphere. To her, life consisted of sun, sea, fine foods and the pleasures of the flesh. The meaning of her life had always resided in her skin and in her belly. Don Francisco had been but another patch of skin to her. It had come as a great shock to Doña Teresa that her husband loved poetry; that he craved music and prayed at night.

Naira left at sunrise and Don Francisco abandoned his tired body to sleep.

From that day forth, a new life began for the two friends. She came to him at night with delicacies gathered from the far corners of the Atacama. He poured the wine and talked about his childhood. He came back from the village with new treats: salami, potatoes, asparagus and the occasional cigar. They whispered in the dark like husband and wife, and in time Don Francisco came to see her as his woman. The ugly hollows in her face became the new moon of her unearthly beauty.

Days, weeks, months flowed by and his love grew steadily, like the formation of a new sand dune.

One evening, he tried to kiss her, but she pulled back in horror.

'I am not a living thing!' she cried. 'My skin is not like yours. My limbs are not like those of the women you have known. If you were to make love to me, you would come to a terrible end. Your days and nights would be spent wandering in the desert; your soul consumed by unspeakable longings.'

'Then let it be so,' said Don Francisco, 'for I want nothing more than to be with you always.'

'You don't know what you are asking!' said Naira—and she fled into the desert.

There followed days of waiting; days in which Don Francisco forgot to eat and drink and refused the comfort of sleep. He sat in his chair, trying once again to conjure memories of his grandmother's tales and was astonished at how little he could remember of his former life. Hovering between hope and despair, he watched as the orange desert light of the mornings gave way to the perilous heat of the afternoons. Nights, the stars hung cool and lonely upon the land. And Don Francisco thought: she will return, indeed she must.

But the days flowed by like a muddy stream and no sign of Naira.

One day, when the pain of waiting lay heavy on his soul, he rode to the village and there walked into the rowdy bar on the plaza, longing to confess his adventure.

'A good day to you, Don Francisco,' said the barman. 'What's your pleasure?'

Don Francisco took a high stool by the counter.

'*Buenos días*, Señor José—I'll have a whiskey and soda.'

The barman frowned. 'Red wine is your usual. Never mind. Whisky and soda it is.'

The barman brought the whiskey and poured in the soda. 'And you're not usually here mid-week. Saturday morning is your visiting time....'

Don Francisco glanced up.

'I suppose it gets lonely out there by the desert,' the barman went on, 'and you know how people talk.'

The barman leaned both elbows on the counter and lowered his voice, 'It's none of my business, but I've heard you're from Valparaiso. So, I wonder what a city person like you is doing out there all alone on that barren land—God's Land as we call it.'

'I have nothing to hide,' Don Francisco replied in a steady voice.

'I never said you did. But what I can't understand is why a man who has lived in a city that has everything— at least, everything a man could desire—would want to come here.'

'Why do they call it God's Land if no one lives there?'

'That's the point: the land is useless. There are no comforts out there, no secure routines to get attached to and no distractions. Then there's the silence and the darkness. It's enough to drive a man crazy! It's not a man's land; it can only be God's Land.'

'Maybe it belongs to the spirits.'

'Spirits?'

'If the land doesn't belong to the living,' Don Francisco offered, 'then maybe it belongs to the dead.'

Presently, Señor José said, 'You don't look like a dead man to me.'

Don Francisco forced a smile and looked about him.

In a corner of the bar, a group of gauchos were playing canasta. From the far end of the hall: the gentle clatter of dominoes. Voices sailed through the air, quiet voices that would now and again break into a guffaw. Drinks were ordered, served, consumed, and conversations hovered over the same ground: who visited whom on which day and what was said or was not said, what did or did not happen.

And Don Francisco thought: I may not look like a dead man, but these men don't look like living creatures.

He swung back to the counter, gulped his whiskey down, thanked Señor José and departed.

At home, he found a letter nailed to his front door. With trembling hands he tore down the letter and devoured its contents.

> *My Dear Don Francisco,*
>
> *When you tried to kiss me I felt the need to protect you from a life more terrible than death. I ran away vowing never to return, but as the days flew by, I felt your waiting and your pain. Your love is lingering in the air, sand, rocks and mountains; a love that has brought new life to my soul.*
>
> *I did not lie to you when I said I was not a living thing. But you must know now that I am not dead either.*

I was born hundreds of years ago, the only daughter to a cruel tyrant and ruler of the Inca. My mother Tamaya lived in fear of my father. When I was four, my mother gave birth to my brother Orco-Varanca and from the moment he was born I sensed his hate for me. Under the old Inca laws a woman may rule. But father wanted Orco-Varanca to be king. My brother lusted for power and plotted my demise. And so, on a day when the clouds were dark and swollen, father and brother did take me to the desert's edge and made me kneel. Binding my legs and arms, they knifed out my eyes. Then, they released me and left me to wander the desert without water. My bones still lie at the edge of the desert—at the foot of the mountain the Indians call Cara de Mujer. My body collapsed, expired and decayed. But I did not die. My longing and desire have left me hovering between life and death.

My father and mother, along with my brother, his children and his children's children have long gone from this earth. And with their deaths, so has my wish for revenge. I want to live. I want to reclaim the life that was my right, not as a ruler of a vanishing nation, but simply as a woman loved.

Yes, I will return to you, Don Francisco. But you must be forewarned of the perils. I

The girl kept her promise: she came to him in the velvet warmth of a New Moon night and made love to him under the vast desert sky. When their love was exhausted, she said, 'I hold your seed within me now, but there is one more act I require you to perform. I need your blood, Don Francisco.'

She held out a knife to him and said, 'This is the knife my father and brother wielded against me. Take it now and use it to give me life.'

Clasping the knife, Don Francisco carved a narrow slit in his left arm and Naira drank greedily from the open wound. Then, lying down on his bed, she let the blood drip over her body, until her lover fell exhausted in her arms.

'Sleep,' she said, as she ran her long silvery fingers over his eyes, 'you must sleep. A long voyage awaits you.'

When he woke the world was black.

'Naira!' he cried, knowing that silence would follow. He fumbled about in his home, searching for the flask of water and the dried meats that he would take with him into the desert. But when he stepped out into the night and realised that the stars had vanished, he was seized by terror. Was he blind? If so, how would he cross the desert? He would need a guide; he would need to borrow a pair of eyes.

Don Francisco stumbled over to his horse, prepared the saddle, and rode out into the Atacama.

After what seemed like days of wandering, he came to the ravine at the foot of *Cara de Mujer*. Dismounting from his horse, he made his way down the steep rocky incline until at length he reached a tangle of thickets of dead trees and bushes. There, in this desolate spot he found a small mound of bones. But where was the girl? Had his journey been in vain? He reached out to caress the remnants of her former life, but the bones crumbled into dust.

All at once, a faint shimmering light emerged from above. Lifting his gaze, Don Francisco beheld Naira at the edge of the ravine. She seemed frail and her body trembled as if she too prepared to crumble into dust. But she was wearing a magnificent silken red robe. And her smiling eyes—yes, she had eyes—were the colour of the earth. He could no longer contain his emotions: breaking into tears and wild sobs, he scrambled out of the ravine and fell exhausted at her feet.

'You kept your promise, Don Francisco,' she said, combing her delicate fingers through his hair. 'Your love brought you to my grave.'

✳

Months later, two men came to Don Francisco's dwelling. They came on horseback, white sombreros on their heads, rifles bulging from their saddles. They dismounted. They searched the house, the well and the land around them.

The tall man was the first to speak.

'Find anything?' he asked his red-haired companion.

'The house is empty. There's no sign of recent activity. The horse is gone, but there are no hoof marks; no indication of where he might have gone.'

'Can you read?'

'Sure. Why do you ask?'

The tall man showed his friend a letter. 'I found this.'

A sandy wind blew in from the desert and the two men had to hold on to their sombreros. When the red-haired man had finished reading, he looked up at his friend.

'Well?' asked the tall man.

The red-haired man remained silent.

'I know, I know. It doesn't make any sense,' the tall man went on, 'but what will we tell the villagers?'

'Señor José swears that Don Francisco talked about going back to Valparaiso.'

'I'd be glad to report that the old city guy went home, but we don't know that for sure.'

'Where else could he have gone?'

The tall man seemed to chew the idea over. 'What about this letter?'

The red-haired man pondered for a moment, then scrunched up the letter and threw it into the well.

They walked back to their horses. The tall man was quick to mount, but his red-haired partner set about rolling a cigarette.

'Hurry up now!' the tall man said, 'I want to get back before nightfall.'

'Hey,' the red-haired man suddenly cried, 'do you suppose Don Francisco wandered out into the desert?'

The tall man lifted his sombrero with one finger and gazed out onto the sun-scorched land. After a moment, he shook his head.

'There's nothing out there—nothing a man could desire.'

THE DEVIL ONLY VISITS

(Chile, circa 1900)

I was on the train to Valparaiso when I met the man with the dog-faced cane and white cravat. I had buried my nose in the morning papers, sprawling in the comfort of a first-class compartment, when, no sooner had I emerged from my leisurely read and thrown down the papers, than I noticed I was not alone. By the open window sat an elderly gentleman, most elegantly attired, with a Roman nose and luminous eyes and skin bronzed by the sun. The pine-scented air that gusted into our compartment ruffled the man's long white hair.

It was midsummer and I had recently taken my priestly vows.

'In a moment, you will see it. There—at the top of the hill,' said the stranger, his eyes wandering out of the window.

I followed his gaze but failed to find what he wanted me to witness. I was troubled that I had not heard him slip into the compartment. True, I had been absorbed in my reading. Even so, I would have heard the carriage door slide open; I would have shifted my legs to let him pass. And his voice! His words seemed to echo deep within his chest. I felt strangely attracted to the man's gentle manners, but was repulsed by the rugged contours of his hands and the faraway look in his eyes.

'You have to know what you're looking for,' he said in a grave voice.

I leaned towards the window and cast my eyes on the rolling hills and there—at the top of a craggy peak—I saw a towering white-stone building. Suddenly, the light vanished as the train plunged into a tunnel, its wheels clattering mercilessly in the darkness. Minutes later, we regained the light of day and I became aware of my fellow traveller fixing me with his cuttlefish eyes. I pondered whether to move to another compartment, but before I could execute my plan, my companion began to lecture me on the history of the region, speaking in a friendly but condescending tone, addressing me as 'Little Father', and on one occasion as 'Your Holiness'.

Most passengers on this route, he said, never notice the old stone building on the hill, which, he went on to explain, was neither a fortress nor a palace, but an abandoned monastery; a desolate place with long halls and vast high-ceilinged rooms that no one dared disturb. It had thrived once under the care of austere, hard-working nuns who had named the place *El Monasterio del Olvido*. Then, an extraordinary thing happened; it was the most mysterious and heart-rending drama that he had ever known. Would I like to hear the story? Valparaiso, that eternal city of magnificent contradictions—as he called it—was still an hour away. Besides, the legend surrounding the monastery was a cautionary lesson on the dangers of prayer, which, as a servant of God, he said, I would find most edifying.

Having passed most of my young life between the walls of the seminary and thus seen so little of the world, the stranger filled me with awe, repugnance and fear. Accordingly: he was irresistible. I remained silent. Fixing me with his staring eyes he began his story.

About 300 years ago, soon after Pedro de Valdivia's visit to Chile and the founding of Santiago, Spanish missionaries built the white-stone refuge which you saw. In those days there were dangers to living in those hills: predators, deadly insects and Indians, who, having acquiesced in the ways of the *conquistadores*, still harboured dreams of revenge. Some of the missionaries died in strange ways and although new priests came to take their place, in time their numbers grew thin. They remained for about 200 years and then mysteriously left. No one knows why or where they went. My own view—I am somewhat of an amateur historian—is that there was something in the land they could not conquer. Nothing tangible, you understand, just a vague resistance, a spirit, perhaps an evil presence that they could not grasp. Then came the war of independence and Chile broke its ties with Spain. The abandoned monastery had, by this time, gained a sinister reputation and no one dared approach the vicinity.

One day, some fifty years ago, two nuns in long grey robes came from beyond the Andes and settled in the monastery. The elder of the two Sisters was short and pale and bent at the shoulders. Her voice was gentle but distant. She gave the impression that all vitality had long gone out of her, as if she were a corpse that had been resuscitated for one last day. Her companion, however, was young: she was tall and thin, with glittering black eyes, long inquisitive fingers and a generous mouth. She addressed her elder as 'Mother' and responded in turn to the name of 'Teresita'.

Who can say what attracted them to the monastery? Perhaps the very hostility of the land or the dark aura of the building presented an irresistible challenge to their faith. When word spread that the monastery was once again inhabited, people from the neighbouring coastal village went to pay their respects to God's new messengers. Would the Sisters be holding mass? Did they require provisions from the village? Imagine these good people's amazement when the Sisters announced that they wanted to be left alone!

'We have come here to forget,' said Mother. 'That is how we serve our Lord. We may, from time to time, descend into your village. But remember: silence and solitude will be our constant companions.'

The villagers were bewildered; they had never known a nun or priest who had not served the people. But the Sisters' wishes were respected and from then on a quiet and distant understanding was established between the village and the monastery.

Two years later, on a spring day full of the smell of sunshine, Teresita made an astounding discovery. She had risen early to go smell the roses that she had planted by the southern wall, and there she saw a shadow lurking in the bushes. Inching her way forward like a puma on the prowl, she stared at the dark hairy thing that was clawing the earth and snarling at the roses.

'It's a wild dog!' Teresita exclaimed, running back to the monastery to fetch Mother.

By the time Teresita returned with Mother, the wild thing had inflicted considerable damage on the rosebushes.

'My roses! He's dug up my roses!'

'That's not a dog,' observed Mother.

'No?'

'No—it's a child. And look: he's hurt.'

Indeed, the intruder was not a wild animal but a male child of about four or five years, with long black hair that trailed down to his waist and hands made rugged from scrounging and scraping. In his frenzied attack on the rose bushes, the child had scratched the crown of his head on the thorns; blood trickled down his face and neck.

Aroused to pity by the sight of the struggling creature, the Sisters lost no time in dragging him into the inner sanctum of the monastery. They tended to his wounds. They fed and clothed him and gave him a cell to sleep in.

Later, as the child lay sleeping in the first bed of his

life, Mother and Teresita debated his future.

'We will have to adopt him,' Teresita said.

'The boy is half-animal,' replied Mother, 'he can't speak.'

'Then we will teach him to speak—and to read and write.'

'It will take more than language to transform this… wild thing into a human being. He will need to read the Gospels, learn to pray, discover the path that God has set for him.'

'And he'll need a name.'

Mother pondered for a moment before replying, 'Yes, I suppose he'll need a good Christian name, such as Juan or Jaime.'

'I shall call him Lobito. After all, he was probably raised by wolves.'

'Teresita! That is not a proper name!'

But the younger Sister asserted her right to name the boy. After all, she had found him. And so the child was adopted and given the name of Lobito—"little wolf".

I'm sure you'll agree that Lobito is not a manly name and certainly not a Christian name. If Mother gave in to Teresita's wish to call the boy so, this was not through weakness or indifference. You see, in a dim corner of the old woman's mind a doubt remained: was the boy truly human? But let us not dwell on Mother's anxieties, or Teresita's affection for the boy, or even what the villagers made of it all. Besides, I'm not here to spin a Gothic tale for your entertainment. I have other, more noble pursuits in mind.

The years passed and Lobito grew into a tall, broad-shouldered youth. Under Teresita's loving guidance he learned to speak and to read and write. In time, he read the Gospels. But his thirst for knowledge extended beyond theology. He devoured books on history, astronomy, botany and the classics of Ancient Greece and Rome. In truth, there was no end to his curiosity. He raised questions that left the Sisters dizzy with wonder; philosophical questions about the beginning and end of all things. Yet he was obedient, placid and serene; his gaze was clear and direct.

One day, as Lobito entered that nebulous territory that lies between the end of childhood and the gates of manhood, Mother posed her question.

'My son, you are a child no longer. The time has come for you to earn your keep.'

'Yes, Mother.'

'Have you thought about your future?'

'Yes, Mother. I will seek work in the village.'

'What kind of work?'

'I will do as the villagers do: I will become a fisherman.'

'And this profession—does it appeal to you?'

'Certainly! Is it not written in the Gospels that Jesus himself was a fisherman?'

Jesus of Nazareth was, of course, a fisherman of souls and not a fisherman of scaly creatures. But Mother approved Lobito's wish and so it was that he went to work upon a trawler that bobbed up and down the coast, day in, day out, whatever the weather. Lobito learned to cast the net and committed to memory the names of all the creatures of the deep. He was often away from the monastery for days at a time, but he always returned loaded with the finest specimens of the Pacific: swordfish, giant hook-clawed crabs, and the king of eels—the *congrio*.

There could be no doubt in the Sisters' minds that Lobito had chosen his profession well. He loved his work. He was happy. Above all, he loved that moment at the end of a long but successful day when fishermen would gather around a beach-fire to tell tales; extraordinary tales of fishing, adventure and romance. And sometimes there were other kinds of stories, told in whispers, about ghosts and evil presences that ruled men's lives; stories that left Lobito perplexed and disoriented. At first, he was able to shrug off their malevolent influence. But when Lobito heard a strange tale about the beautiful-corrupt city of Valparaiso, the worm of doubt began gnawing at his faith.

The old man had fallen silent. His gaze flew out of the window and onto the mountains. Thinking that he had suddenly and without reason forgotten my presence, I sprang to my feet and laid my hand on the sliding door. I was about to make my escape when I heard his deep commanding voice calling me to attention.

'Be seated, Little Father!' he cried, 'I have not yet finished with you.'

I had always been a stubborn youth, always demanded of life that it should conform to my wishes and ideas. So it came as a great surprise when, against my will, I returned to my seat. I felt gripped by an unknown force, as if an invisible boa were crushing my capacity for decisive acts. I tried to speak, but my tongue lay inert in my mouth like a desiccated slug.

'I find it surprising,' said the stranger, 'that a man of God should be so lacking in patience! Have I bored you? Yes, that's probably it: I have rambled and digressed. I have strayed from the Biblical forms of storytelling that you are familiar with. Very well, I shall get to the point. But mark my words, Little Father, I'm not telling you this story to pass the time. No! It is the advancement of your soul that interests me.'

Fixing me once again with his fathomless eyes, the stranger continued with his story.

And so—one day, when a warm mist had settled on the trawler, Lobito caught a strange creature. It was a crab, but one the likes of which had never been seen before. Large, grey, with luminous eyes, it seemed to Lobito that all his doubts and fears had come to him in the shape of this ugly creature from the depths of the Pacific. Disgusted with his catch, he threw the vile crustacean into the ocean. But he could not shake off the troublesome thought that had come to him all at once. He returned to shore and walked away from the beach in long despairing strides. Arriving at the monastery, he made his way to Mother's study, passing Teresita without word or greeting.

Mother saw at once that Lobito was troubled in his inmost soul.

'What is it, my son? What ails you?'

'Mother, I have lost my serenity. I have heard strange tales of evil and monstrous things.'

'Stories! Is that how you spend your time: in idle chatter and gossip?'

'Mother—hear me out. It has never been my way to heed the tales of the good folk of the village. But when I heard fishermen whispering the name of Lucifer, I was besieged by doubt. You have taught me to be a good Christian. Accordingly, I believe in God. But I cannot accept the existence of the Devil.'

'Lobito, my son, if your faith in God is, as you claim, firm and strong, you must necessarily believe in the existence of God's enemy.'

'But if God is all-powerful—as you have taught me—why not create a universe without suffering; a world where we would not be tempted by the sly arguments of an Evil One?'

Lobito's question was like a breeze that forebodes a powerful storm; Mother did not know what to do or say; she turned her back on the youth and stared out of the window.

'I have unsettled you,' said Lobito. 'Perhaps I should leave.'

Mother whirled about. 'What is this talk about leaving?'

'Mother, I know you believe in Lucifer. But I must grapple with my doubts in my own way: I must find this terrible angel of darkness. I must see him with my own eyes.'

'Have you taken leave of your senses?' Mother exclaimed in a quivering voice. 'Even if I were to agree to your wild scheme, where do you propose to search for him?'

Lobito now surprised the old woman by recounting the strange tale he had hear from the fishermen.

Once upon a time—they had told him—long before men and women walked along our shores, the Devil was cast out of God's kingdom and thrown at the foot of the Andes. He wandered about until he came to the hills that would one day become Valparaiso. He marvelled at the splendour of the blue Pacific, vast and indomitable. Wherever he looked, the Devil saw incomparable beauty—and it reminded him of God. And because he had once loved the Lord with all his heart, he wept for years without respite; and the tears that fell to the ground, full of the poison of revenge, burned the flowers and the grass. The barren ground upon the hill where the Devil shed his tears is now his home. The people of Valparaiso say, always in a whisper, that the Devil resides by the harbour; that he lives in a mansion made of lapis lazuli; and that he strolls along the waterfront in his magnificent white suit and dog-faced cane.

A beautiful story, don't you agree Little Father? Of course, this is folklore, not the Gospels. But deep within Lobito's soul he wondered whether there might be a drop of truth to the old folk tale. Consequently— for his own peace of mind—he decided to investigate the matter.

58

As you can imagine, Mother did all she could to persuade Lobito to remain at the monastery, but she soon discovered the futility of all argument. And when Teresita heard that her *hermano* was leaving for the city, she climbed the highest tower of the monastery and there, like Dido of Carthage, she watched him as he made his way, suitcase in hand, to the nearest railway station.

Thus, Lobito took the train to Valparaiso, winding his way on this very same route that we are journeying on now. Who can say? Perhaps he boarded this train; maybe he sat in this very compartment or even in the seat that you are occupying right now.

Lobito sank back into the plush leather seat of a first-class compartment and allowed his thoughts to meander. He had filled his suitcase with clean shirts and a small bottle of eau de cologne. Inexplicably, he believed that city people looked eternally clean and smelled of flowers, unlike the villagers whose hands were always dirty and their nails perpetually broken. So he decided that he too would look clean and smell fresh during his visit to the ancient port. In his imagination, he painted Lucifer as a polite gentleman, elegant and well spoken, clean and perfumed. There could be no doubt that the city was the natural environment for a devil. Besides, there were no books in the monastery that he could consult; and if Lucifer's evil activities had been documented throughout the centuries, then the records of his achievements would be found in the archives of the old library at the Catholic University of Valparaiso.

As he mused along these lines he fell into a deep slumber. Hours later, he awoke, and his eyes were captivated by the presence of an elderly gentleman sitting by the window, a crafty smile wandering on his lips.

'Permit me to introduce myself,' said the old man, 'I am Don Lucca. May I inquire what business calls you to Valparaiso? Perhaps I may be of service to you.'

Examining the old man with a critical eye, Lobito saw at once that Don Lucca was a man who dressed with great care. Moreover, his protruding nose and rich white hair reassured him: here was a man who had seen the world and who could guide him. He lost no time in revealing to Don Lucca his conversation with Mother and the painful question that was taking him to Valparaiso.

'So you wish to prove the existence of the Devil?' Don Lucca asked, without a trace of surprise. 'If you'll permit me to make a suggestion, I believe—I am somewhat of an amateur theologian—I believe that the answer that you seek can be found in the mystical works of the great Carmelite, San Juan de la Cruz. He was, as you know, a saint and one of the greatest of all Christian poets. Let us, therefore, investigate this matter together. Oh, please, there's no need to thank me. Besides, I have a special interest in this matter. I am, one could say, a patron of the Catholic library. Yes, I will see to it that you are given copies of all of San Juan's works.'

Lobito thanked the old man ceremoniously.

Upon arriving at Valparaiso, they lost no time in wending their way through the gloomy labyrinths of the age-worn city. Night had fallen and the inquisitive moon glimmered gently on the harbour. Bitter smells lingered in the air; whispering shadows darted through the narrow streets and deserted squares. At length they reached the library, a magnificent building with tall, ponderous gates of dark wood. Naturally, the library was closed. But in his worldly innocence, Lobito showed no amazement when Don Lucca extracted a large ring of keys from his pocket, and, unlocking the enormous doors, he led our hero into the interior of the house of knowledge. They marched through large rooms with low ceilings connected by long narrow passageways; tomb-like rooms brimming with damp-stained books. Finally, they arrived at a melancholy corner of the library where they became absorbed in examining some old tomes.

In the days and nights that followed, Lobito pored over the books that Don Lucca brought to him and learned of the pain and solitude that accompanies the true spiritual path. He surrendered to the words of San Juan as to the arms of a beloved. Captivated by the promise of a life beyond this world, he became ab-sorbed in the vision of a spiritual home that Mother had withheld from him. The books became his universe and the library his home. He forgot his former life and the strange tales of the fishermen. Even the memory of his beloved Teresita receded to the far reaches of his mind, until the day came when he had read all there was to read and he searched for Don Lucca, to ask his advice.

He found the old man in a windowless section of the library, where the lights were dim. Don Lucca looked tired and haggard but he was, as always, impeccably dressed. His long white jacket seemed to light up the shadows and his silk shirt was without a crease.

When old Lucca saw Lobito, he bowed to his young friend and said, 'What is it that you are carrying?'

Lobito handed him a book. 'I beg you, Don Lucca. There is a passage in this book that I would like you to read. I have marked the page.'

'He fled into the desert where men could not reach him,' Don Lucca began. 'He travelled to a forgotten land where words were not spoken, and all was darkness. He carried his spiritual treasures in his heart; the harvest of his prayers, and searched for the infinite caverns where God dwelt. But there was an Evil upon him that pursued him into the wilderness.'

'Please go on.'

'For he who gathers the gifts of God unto himself,' continued the old man, 'arouses the envy of the Fallen Angel. And the loss of one refined soul is more painful to the Evil One than the loss of many sinners.'

'What does all this mean, Don Lucca?'

'It is an obscure text, I grant you, but the message is clear: the Devil only visits souls who are close to God.'

That's right Little Father: Evil only comes to those who search for Good. Surely, you must have learned this in the seminary. No? Ah well, it is the Church's best-kept secret. Paradoxical as it may seem, the human search for purity destroys goodness, and our sins—alas!—redeem us. We all know of the power and the rewards of prayer. But the early Christians—St. Antony, Evagrius Ponticus, Isaac of Nineveh—they knew also of its perils. Ah, I see that my words have fired your theological imagination. Stop squirming! I hate it when you fidget and wriggle about. Besides, you distract me and I have not yet finished recounting Lobito's perilous odyssey into his own soul.

That night, Lobito awoke screaming from a dream.

He had journeyed to the Holy Land and seen the Christ upon the cross, alive and in pain. He had wanted to help the suffering man by removing the nails from the wounded hands and feet; but upon the crucified man's knee there perched a small dark crab, its pincers digging deep into skin. Two more crabs were crawling up his legs and soon the image of the Christ was swallowed by the vision of a thousand crabs upon his body. It was a terrifying dream and upon awakening Lobito knew that his time in Valparaiso had come to an end.

One evening, and several weeks after Lobito's departure, the Sisters were returning from one of their rare visits to the village. No sooner had they entered the monastery than they were seized by indescribable sensations. Making their way into the interior of the forbidding refuge, they heard sounds both ominous and intriguing. The shuffling of feet—metal scraping wood—hammering and pounding, followed by stillness.

'It's Lobito!' Teresita cried. 'He's returned!'

Yes, Lobito had returned, but the Sisters could not reach him. Acting on his newfound knowledge, Lobito had locked and bolted the entrance to his cell, and boarded the windows so that no light could penetrate within. The Sisters gathered outside his cell, wondering at his self-imprisonment. Oh, they pounded the door and called his name; they demanded an explanation for his inexplicable behaviour. But all of their efforts were met by silence.

Suddenly, Mother turned to Teresita and said, 'Quick! Run to the village and seek help. We must prise him out his cell.'

Perhaps Teresita realized what fate had in store for her *hermano*, for, without questioning Mother's command, she plunged into the night and headed for the village.

Meanwhile, paying no heed to Mother's pleas to emerge from his cell, Lobito began to pray. He prayed with a passion that surprised him. He prayed that his former self might die so that he could be resurrected to a new life. He prayed so that he might forget the world and know only the will of God. He prayed with fervour and despair, fear and guilt.

As night settled on the monastery, Lobito pursued his solitary path into prayer. Later, as the light of a new day brought warmth to the land, he heard fists pounding at his door and the voices of the villagers calling him to come forth from his tomb. But the voices seemed like faint and desperate calls from an unknown land. And in his fever for a vision of a world beyond his own, the mystical world of San Juan, Lobito fled inwards where words could not reach him. Without heed for the hunger and thirst that lay siege to his body, he continued to pray, until at length, overcome by a profound weariness of the soul, he took himself to bed and slept.

When he opened his eyes it was dark. A vast stillness lay upon the world, like an omen of an unspeakable fear that was soon to possess him. He heard the wind shrieking in the night, a rhythmic calling that was hypnotic and strange. All at once, his limbs became rigid and his tongue turned heavy as stone. And he struggled against the invisible grip that held him, unable to accept that this was the moment that he had been waiting for.

A man in a monk's cowl stood at the foot of the bed. And as Lobito looked upon the inner features of the stranger's countenance, he saw beauty and brutality, power and temptation. Here was the mystery of the ultimate corruption, alluring and seductive, but beyond what the human mind could endure. To his horror, he saw the stranger's arms out-stretched, the long fingers of both hands entwined around his knees. And as the stranger's grip grew tighter and the air congealed into foulness, he fought to speak the words that would dispel the brooding stillness that coiled about his body. But the only sounds that lingered in the air were the echoes of his bones breaking in the dark…

The train had come to an abrupt halt and I, who feared the journey would never end, felt bewildered and—strange to admit—forlorn. For as much as I detested the old man, he had exerted a fascination on my mind.

At last, the spell was broken: I jumped to my feet, peered out the window and looked along the length of the train. Men and women darted up and down the platform, hauling their suitcases and calling out to porters. Workmen in grimy shirts loaded and unloaded parcels; uniformed officials inspected the passengers' papers; horse-drawn carriages came and went.

So this was Valparaiso! But the light in the station was a strange and luminous grey: I could not have said whether it was dawn or twilight. Then, I wheeled around and looked at the old man as he rose to his feet. Gathering his white panama and dog-faced cane, he brushed the dust off his immaculate white jacket and said, 'Well, Little Father, I hope your stay in Valparaiso will be a pleasant one. Perhaps we will meet again. If so, let us share a drink and watch the sun as it falls asleep in the harbour. Or discuss theology. After all, you and I, we're not so very different.'

So saying, the old man gave me a magnanimous bow, turned about, and walked away. I watched him as he stepped off the train and vanished in the crowd.

Suddenly, it occurred to me that the old man had made up that wild story about the monastery; that he had been pulling my leg all along and had taken me for a gullible fool. I could believe that the Devil roamed the treacherous streets of Valparaiso; I might even accept that there were hidden dimensions to prayer. But that the Devil should go about breaking the kneecaps of good Christians...!

COLONEL REDL'S KNIFE SHEATH

I

IN the autumn of 1941 I left my home in Basel to spend quiet days in Gandria, a remote village carved into the Swiss Alpine cliff that overlooks the southern arm of Lake Lugano. German troops had crossed the Russian border; the Red Army was outflanked; the siege of Leningrad had just begun. And although I lived in a peaceful island amidst a sea of brutalities, the thought of the millions that were destined to die weighed heavy on my mind.

I took a room in the only hotel in the village—a modest place run by a Spanish widow, a woman in her sixties with melancholic dark eyes and a deep-set jaw who, however, was an excellent cook. She had another quality that, in my despondent state of mind, proved to be a gift from heaven: she had little interest in her guests, and her questions were confined to inquiring whether I had slept well or if the meal had pleased me. And so I spent my days wandering along the lake, breathing in the odour of pine and rosemary, and thinking only of my next meal.

There was one other guest at the hotel, a man of about fifty-five or fifty-six, immaculately dressed at all times, who exuded an air of refinement and knowledge. But I soon learned that he too wanted to be left alone, and indeed, although we saw each other at breakfast, lunch and dinner, we made a ritual of eating at separate tables with only the occasional nod of recognition exchanged between us.

One night, the warm damp air pressed down upon my breath such that my bedroom seemed to be shrinking to intolerable proportions. At last, I gave up the struggle for sleep. I wandered down the stairs and onto the long balcony that looked onto the lake. There, I spied my lonely companion sitting at a small table, absorbed in his thoughts. As I had no wish to intrude upon the man's intimate solitude, I turned to make my exit. Suddenly, he saw me, and to my astonishment, he rose and greeted me.

'I hope you will not think me a bad host,' he said. 'Will you join me? I have just opened a bottle of Barolo.'

His speech was accompanied by elegant gestures that gave the impression of old-fashioned manners. I was charmed and intrigued by his invitation; I sat at his table and accepted the glass of deep-red wine. Now that I was sitting close to the man, I took a moment to study his features. Despite his middle age he was dark and handsome. A grim determination pervaded his jaw and forehead; but his hands were restless, suggesting a peculiar nervousness or premonitory fear.

'You strike me as a wanderer,' I said at last, 'or a homeless scholar.'

He laughed heartily. 'I certainly enjoy my own company and I'm also something of a modern Odysseus. But I have never sought knowledge or erudition. I'm afraid you've misjudged me.'

'So you are a man of action?'

'Once upon a time, yes—but what about you?'

'I often wonder about the futility of all action,' I said with profound sadness.

'The futility of all action: an intriguing idea. Perhaps you are the person I have been seeking...'

I shot him an inquiring glance.

'I have wandered the continent and lived in many countries,' he went on, 'but my search has been guided by one aim only: to find a confessor. I've been observing you for some days and I feel an unaccountable compulsion to tell you my story.'

I turned my gaze to the moon's silvery light rippling on the lake. I had come to Gandria to escape all tales of death and destruction. Yet, against my will, I felt sympathy for my unknown companion of the night. Taking my silence as acquiescence, he embarked on a long story—the strangest tale of guilt I ever heard.

II

My name is Ebinger—Carl Josef Ebinger; and I am a native of Vienna.

I completed my military training in 1909; a year later I joined the Intelligence Bureau of the Imperial and Royal Army. My commanding officer and trainer was Colonel Alfred Redl. No doubt, you are familiar with the name: I am referring to the Colonel Redl who was decorated with the Order of the Iron Cross for his outstanding services to Austrian Intelligence and who, perhaps, became the most brilliant military officer of his generation. I might add that Colonel Redl was the most humorous, kind and gentle officer I ever met—a graceful, elegant and compassionate person who launched me on my career and acted as a mentor and spiritual father to me.

In 1912 I was appointed to the rank of Detective Sergeant. But my story really begins in the spring of 1913, when, together with Detective Sergeant Steidl, I was assigned to a mysterious case, one that had baffled Austrian and German counter-espionage agencies since 1911: someone in Austrian Intelligence was relaying vital military secrets to Russia. But there were as yet no clues with which to launch an investigation.

Then—it was in April 1913—we got our first lucky break. A letter arrived at Vienna's General Delivery Office on Fleischmarkt Square, addressed to a certain Herr Nizetas. The postmark was from Berlin and as the letter went unclaimed, it was returned to Berlin, where it was opened by German secret police. At that time Germany and Austria were in agreement to exchange information that might be crucial to the security of both countries. On inspecting the contents of the letter, German police concluded that it was imperative to contact Austrian Intelligence; for the envelope contained 6000 kronen and two addresses—one in Switzerland, the other in France—addresses which had, moreover, been identified as contact points for Russian spies.

This was the break that we had been waiting for and Austrian Intelligence conceived a plan that was brilliant in its simplicity. The letter was resealed with its contents intact and returned to General Delivery. Detective Sergeant Steidl and I were appointed to stake out the post office; we took up residence in a small room across the square. We waited and watched. Sooner or later the recipient of the letter would turn up. We had instructed the post manager: as soon as Herr Nizetas collected his letter, he was to contact us by means of an electric bell whose wire ran from under the counter of the post office right into our room.

Days, weeks trickled by and Herr Nizetas did not appear. Meanwhile, two more letters arrived in his name. We opened both letters and found 6000 kronen in one and 8000 in the other, along with mysterious notes that did not further our knowledge of the case. But the new letters gave us an incentive to continue our long siege. We resealed the new letters and returned them to the post office.

Six weeks later, a few minutes before six o'clock on the evening of May 24 1913, our patience was rewarded in a way we could not have foreseen.

When my mind flies back to that magnanimous day, I remember details which, over the years, have taken on an importance that I cannot fathom. I remember that it was a Saturday evening and a cold one at that. It was the coldest May evening that I can recall, and yet, it was a clear day with a sky so blue it had the effect of mesmerising me into forgetfulness. I remember also that, for once, we had not been expecting anything to happen. But it did. The bell rang and we nearly missed it. Steidl had gone downstairs to relieve his bladder, while I had gone to the kitchen to prepare coffee. So when the bell sounded there was only an empty room to greet its warning. Steidl had just emerged from the privy and I was carrying my cup of coffee in one hand when we met in the corridor and heard the bell ringing through the door. The cup slipped from my grasp and splintered on the floor, coffee splashing my shoes and staining my trousers.

We shot down the stairs, bolted out the building and raced across the square, arriving at the post office with our arms flapping. Herr Nizetas had arrived, yes, but he had already departed. We ran outside in time to see a cab speeding around the corner and I was granted a miraculous fraction of a second in which to make a mental note of the license number—A3313. There was a moment of near-silence between Steidl and I; the only sound to reach our ears was the sound of our rapid breaths.

'We have him!' Steidl exclaimed.

'Our man has got away!' I cried.

'But we have the cab number. We can track him wherever he goes.'

'It may be hours before we find the cab and by then—who can say where our fugitive will be? We don't even know what he looks like.'

We ran back to the post office and quizzed the clerk for vital clues, but there was little in the way of information. Herr Nizetas had entered General Delivery wearing a hat pulled over his face so that it had been impossible for the clerk to get a glimpse of the man's features. The hat itself was a typical one—of medium brim—and the man's height was medium too. The man's voice had no distinguishing characteristics: a typical male voice with a typical Viennese accent. In brief, we had nothing to go on and nothing to show for our six weeks of waiting.

As we walked out of the post office my mind was already working on an explanation to give headquarters for our failure to catch our man. Imagine our surprise when, upon exiting onto the square, we saw a cab rolling along with the license plate A3313! We lost no time in hailing the cab and showering the driver with questions. Our emotions had run away with us: we were screaming and gesticulating, pushing our badges into the driver's face. All these emotional expressions on our part only served to astonish the driver and delay our search. When the driver had finally understood what we wanted, he informed us that the gentleman that we were searching for had not gone very far: he had stopped a few blocks away at the Café Kaiserhof. And it seemed that the passenger had been anxious to get there as soon as possible, for in his haste he had left the sheath of a penknife with which he had used to open the letters.

We confiscated the sheath and made our rapid way towards the café and within minutes we were facing what seemed like another dead end. The headwaiter assured us that no one had entered the Kaiserhof in the last fifteen minutes. But having got this far we were not going to admit defeat without a struggle. We began asking questions, and, as chance would have it, a cab driver waiting outside was able to identify our man. A gentleman with a grey hat over his face had got out of one cab and immediately into another and had asked to be taken to Hotel Klomser.

At Hotel Klomser we asked the concierge to direct us to Herr Nizetas.

'I'm afraid I can't help you, gentlemen,' he said, 'we have no one staying with us by that name. And I can assure you that I always remember our visitors' names.'

'Has anyone come into the hotel in the last half hour?' asked Steidl.

'Yes, certainly—at least half a dozen persons have asked for their keys. We are a very busy—'

'We need the names of everyone who has entered the hotel in the last thirty minutes,' I commanded.

'Well, if it's absolutely necessary…about half hour ago Herr Felsen asked for his keys, as well as two ladies. What were their names? Ah yes, there was Frau Kleinemann, who is the wife of Bank President

Kleinemann, with Frau Lüchow, who is married to Director—'

'Forget the ladies,' I snapped, '—we're just interested in the men.'

'I see. Well, after Felsen there was Herr Doctor Widener and Professor Zank and Colonel Redl…'

When Steidl and I heard that name we gave each other a significant look, but I was the first to recover my wits.

'Did you say Colonel Redl?'

'Yes.'

'Colonel *Alfred* Redl?'

'I don't understand why you find that surprising. Colonel Redl has stayed with us before. In fact, he always stays with us when he arrives from Prague and always in Room One.'

'Let's talk to Redl,' Steidl suggested, 'I'm sure he'll be able to clear up this coincidence.'

I turned to Steidl and gave him a severe look. 'We're under strict instructions to consult no one except our contact at headquarters. Besides, we need to determine for ourselves whether Colonel Redl…'

I couldn't finish the sentence.

Steidl and I stood gazing at each other for some time before we recovered our composure and made further enquiries of the concierge. We soon learned from him that Colonel Redl had entered the hotel in civilian clothes some fifteen minutes earlier, holding a grey hat in one hand. He had asked for his keys and gone up to his room. As the concierge assured us that

Colonel Redl always dined out in the evenings, we decided to wait in the hotel lobby.

'When the Colonel comes down,' I instructed the concierge, 'would you ask him if he has lost this knife sheath?'

An hour later, we spied the Colonel as he came down the stairs, dressed in his officer's uniform and with a well-groomed moustache. As he handed his keys at reception the concierge carried out our orders.

'Good evening, Herr Colonel. Did you, by any chance, misplace your knife sheath?'

'Why yes, as a matter of fact, I was looking for it only a moment ago,' said Redl, reaching for the sheath.

At that moment, I witnessed the gesture that has haunted my life ever since. The Colonel's hand hovered over the knife sheath like a bird of prey that senses a trap. All at once, he pulled back his hand as if he had been burned by the Trojan gift. He glanced at the concierge and swung round and swept the lobby with fearful eyes. Then, with bowed head, he walked out of the hotel.

'He didn't take it,' said Steidl.

I shook my head. 'His hand betrayed him. Colonel Redl *is* Herr Nizetas.'

Steidl and I realized that we had to act fast; a decision would have to be taken about Colonel Redl that same evening. And it was a painful decision for us to make. You see, Colonel Redl had trained us; he had made us what we were; he embodied all that was worthy and respectable about our profession. Colonel Redl had betrayed his country, yet Steidl and I experienced his betrayal as if it had been directed at our very souls. Thus, we contacted headquarters at eight o'clock and two hours later the course of history had been forged. When Colonel Redl returned from dinner and asked the concierge for his keys, he was approached by four men who requested to speak with him on an urgent matter.

I was one of those four men.

The Colonel invited us to his room and there we sat and discussed his dealings with Russian Intelligence. At first, he denied our accusations, speaking in an agitated fashion. But when I pulled the knife sheath from out of my jacket, I saw him turn pale and weak. Shortly before midnight Colonel Redl resigned himself to the inevitable: he admitted his guilt. We made it clear that in the interest of public morale and the honour of the military, it was imperative that his actions remained a secret. And so, we struck a deal: we promised to preserve his honourable name in exchange for his immediate signed confession and self-execution. Accordingly, we left the Colonel's room at one in the morning, leaving a loaded revolver and his knife sheath on a small mahogany table by his side.

Twenty minutes later, the concierge brought me a confidential message in the form of a sheet of paper folded in a triangle and carried on a silver tray—it was from Redl. I read the message in the lobby and reflected on the wisdom of a private parley with the Colonel. At length, I made my way to Room One, knocked once and entered.

Colonel Redl was sitting in the armchair where I had left him. A cigarette was balanced delicately between the second and third fingers of his trembling left hand.

'What do you want?' I said, in a hostile tone.

'I want to warn you against the sin of pride, or, as the ancient Greeks called it—Hubris. I take it you have read Herodotus?'

'I didn't have the privilege of a classical education.'

'In that case, let me refer you to Book One, Chapter Thirty-Two of *The Histories*. It's the section in which Croesus, the king of Lydia, demands to know of Solon why he holds happiness in such contempt.'

Crushing his cigarette in an ashtray the Colonel continued, 'And Solon replies that anyone who lives for a long time will sooner or later experience forces beyond his control. Placing the limit of a man's life at seventy years, Solon calculates that such a life comes to 26,250 days.'

'Is there a point to your little history lesson?'

'Ah, spoken like a true Croesus. As a matter of fact, the point is plain for anyone to see: since no two days bring with them events that are exactly the same, it follows that human life is entirely determined by chance.'

'So?'

'So, if I do not congratulate you for discovering my secret activities, it is because in this matter of spy against spy you have been favoured by a series of lucky breaks and nothing more.'

All at once, the Colonel leapt to his feet and shot me a defiant glance.

He went on, 'If you want to know how I feel about this moment, in which I stand at the brink of the end—I feel relieved. Yes, relieved that I no longer have to live like a hunted animal. Oh, I behaved foolishly—like a gambler on a winning streak who keeps betting, all along knowing that it cannot last. Well, if there is one lesson that spying has taught me, it is that the individual is always crushed in the end.'

'Herr Colonel, I was under the impression that you called me to make one last request.'

'Yes, that is still my intention. I want you to give me your word of honour that you will do all you can to defend my good name.'

'But—we have already agreed on this!'

'We have made a formal agreement—that is correct. But I do not trust the other officers who came here tonight. I trust you Ebinger, and I'm asking you for the sake of our old friendship if you will give me your word of honour to preserve my reputation as an Imperial Officer.'

We were standing close to each other; I could feel Redl's breath; I saw the faint quiver of his lower lip and—I gave my word of honour. No sooner had I made my promise than a strange, elusive feeling of disquietude assailed my being. But I could not give this emotion a name.

Suddenly, the Colonel thrust an object into my hands and said, 'I believe this belongs to you now.'

I saw to my horror that he had forced the knife sheath into my grasp. I looked up at him and there, written on his countenance, was an expression I had never seen before, but one that I now recognize as infinite despair. Then, with brutal swiftness he grabbed me by the shoulder with one hand—with the other he flung open the door—then he hurled me into the hallway.

I heard the slam of the door and the click of the lock.

Several hours later, and shortly before sunrise, a shot rang out from Room One: Colonel Redl had kept his side of the bargain.

III

If you had bought the *Neue Freie Presse* on Monday, May 26 1913, you would have perused on its front page a series of articles discussing the tension between Serbia and Bulgaria, as well as a long and detailed account of the wedding ceremony of Kaiser Wilhelm's daughter to Prince Ernst August von Braunschweig. But you would have had to turn the page to read the short paragraph announcing Colonel Redl's death from a gunshot to the mouth. The Colonel was described as a talented officer on the verge of a great career; a man who had gained popularity in the military; but a man who had been suffering from mental overexertion and severe neurasthenia. There were no other details—not even the name of the hotel where he had met his end.

I wish I could tell you that the story of Colonel Redl's treachery ended in this quiet manner. It had been my intention to spread a mantle of respectability over Redl's painful deeds. It is my great regret that there was one event I overlooked; if my attention had

80

not wavered at that critical moment, the course of history would have flowed along a different path. This is how it happened.

I had left the Colonel's room at about two o'clock, but hours went by before he swallowed the fatal bullet. In that time, the Colonel must have paced his room and looked back upon his life. When a man surveys his life he oftentimes reflects on the persons he has loved. Our love is embodied in the objects that we treasure and seek to preserve from the ravages of time: letters, photographs, gifts. In those silent hours between our ultimate conversation and his death, Colonel Redl brought forth the private embodiments of his many loves and left them for the world to see.

At sunrise and in another part of the city, a locksmith named Hans Wagner was preparing to play halfback for the Club Sturm soccer team against another amateur team, the Club Union Holleschowitz. But the match was scheduled to take place a hundred and thirty miles northwest of Vienna. Wagner was about to leave his home and make his way to the Westbahnhof when a convoy of soldiers arrived at his front door and commanded him to accompany them to Hotel Klomser. Having gathered his tools, he was thrown into a military car and driven at an unprecedented speed across Vienna to the hotel where I was standing guard to Room One.

'Force the lock,' I said to Wagner when he arrived, 'but be quick and do as little damage as possible.'

He was an efficient little man this Hans Wagner, for he forced the lock with a minimum of effort and at

lightning speed. I was the first to dash into the room;
the first to see the lifeless body of the man who had
been my mentor; I was the first to glimpse the secret
current of Redl's past—for scattered across the room
were bizarre objects: heavily-perfumed garments,
photographs depicting men in erotic poses, hair dyes,
scents, cosmetics and letters—love letters—that revealed all. I gave orders to my men to remove the body
and commanded the concierge to gather the strange
objects littered about the room into one bundle. On
everyone I impressed the need for secrecy.

Suddenly, a vague feeling of something-not-quite-
right began to oppress me.

'Where's Wagner?' I asked a soldier standing at the
door.

'He's gone, Sir.'

'Why did you let him leave?'

'We only brought him to break the lock. I
thought—'

'You blundering fool!' I cried.

I plunged out of the room, raced down the stairs
and out into the street—Wagner had vanished. Would
he speak about what he had seen? I reassured myself
that even if he were to reveal what he had witnessed,
it would never amount to more than a cheap rumour.

The next day Wagner paid a visit to Egon Kisch,
the captain of the Club Sturm soccer team, and gave
his apologies for having missed the match. He also
surrendered an explanation for his absence. Kisch was
in a foul mood, for Club Sturm, a strong team and the
favourite to win, had lost to the challengers and Kisch

waved the blame at Wagner. At first, Kisch threatened to throw Wagner out of his office, but as the locksmith insisted in giving his account of the strange call-out to Hotel Klomser, the captain gradually became pacified.

To Wagner's surprise, Kisch extracted a notebook from his jacket and began taking copious notes and asking questions.

'So, the man who shot himself was in uniform?'

'Yes. It was an officer's uniform. You know: sky-blue with gold choke collar, three stars…'

'A Colonel! Wait a moment…' said Kisch, flicking through the pages of the *Neue Freie Presse*.

Kisch was a shrewd investigator and it didn't take long for him to gather the pieces of this mystery. True, he couldn't be sure that the man who had died at Hotel Klomser was Colonel Redl, but Kisch was also a professional journalist and he knew how to tease the truth out of the most unpromising materials. Realizing that Redl's obituary was a carefully crafted narrative lie, he wrote his own very subversive account and published it in a Berlin newspaper. Before long, questions were being raised at all levels, like hound dogs in pursuit of an elusive fox.

Three days later, on May 29, 1913, the War Ministry was forced to print a new official statement of events in the *Military Review*: Colonel Redl had been in severe financial difficulties for several years because of his outlandish homosexual activities. Moreover, Austrian Intelligence could now confirm that Colonel Redl had sold official secret information to a foreign power.

The revelation that Colonel Redl had betrayed his country sent scandal scurrying through every echelon and corner of the military; and shame descended on the Austrian nation like the plagues of biblical lore. In time, it became apparent that Redl's career as a spy for Russia had extended some ten years and that his name would be chiselled into the pantheon of the greatest traitors that history would ever know. Egon Kisch's ruthless investigations uncovered the horrific facts that Redl had informed the Russians of Austria's military designs on Serbia; that he had given false accounts of Russia's military plans to the Austrian generals; and that all these actions had brought death to hundreds of thousands of Austrians.

I could supply you with the names of those who were crushed under the weight of this national disaster, from Redl's lover, Lieutenant Stefan Hromadka, who was found guilty of unnatural sexual practices, to Colonel von Urbanski, chief of the Intelligence Bureau, who was forced to take early retirement. What matters are not the minor casualties that swept the military but the verdict that history would pronounce if my story ever came to light; for if there was one person who could have spared Austria the moral catastrophe that Colonel Redl had set in motion, that person was none other than Detective Sergeant Ebinger.

In recognition of my guilt I have carried Colonel Redl's knife sheath with me all these long years and I carry it still. I know you have been watching me; now and then you have caught me looking at some object that I pull from out of my jacket. No, it's not a book, not a wallet, not a diary. It's a battered piece of leather in worn-out beige and despite its age you can still distinguish the letter R stamped in red on its back. I carried that knife sheath on the day I offered my resignation in June 1913—a resignation that was rejected. An Imperial order arrived granting me unlimited leave to reflect upon my decision and after months of wandering the gloomy streets of Vienna, I left home never to return.

Of my life from that day forth there is not a single event worthy of recounting; I have travelled the continent like the Wandering Jew of legend. As for Redl's knife sheath, it is the only material possession that links me to Austria's past; it is the sole remaining visible manifestation of the person I once was. And now, as I approach the end of my story, I fear you might extend me a word of kindness; that you might attempt to appease my guilt; or that you might wield logic to demonstrate that Austria's downfall was not my doing. I beg you—do not speak! Still, I have one last request to make of you: that you sit here with me a moment longer. The sun will soon be climbing over that mountain peak—there—and the light, you'll see, will dart across the lake, painting red and orange waves in a conflagration of startling beauty, the kind of beauty that jolts the soul into forgetfulness. Perhaps I may forget my tragic past for a breath or two; and together we may forget that beyond the mountains war still rages.

THE POSSESSED

ON the day my mother died the rain pounded the earth. I heard a cry like the wailing of a wild beast; and I ran up the stairs and caught a glimpse of my mother lying on her bedroom floor. Father was standing over her inert body; his shoulders stooped like the wings of a buzzard. When I made to enter, father came out and blocked my path. He shut the door behind him and stood like a sentry on duty. I reached for the doorknob. But father said, 'Harry, my boy, if you don't go to your room, so help me God, I will knock you flat out.'

I knew father was averse to cuffing; but he was a man of his word.

I was fourteen at that time. Father and I were living in a small Edwardian house on a quiet square just a short stroll from Kew. Mother died on a Thursday and the rain continued into Tuesday. She was buried without ceremony on the Wednesday morning. To be sure, the priest came to give his blessing; and behind him stood the gravedigger, shovel in hand. The rain had stopped, but a thin sad drizzle permeated the air.

We all helped lower mother into her resting place; but father forbade me watch as the grave was sealed with earth.

When we reached home father led me into his study and bade me stand by the door. He walked over to his desk and found his silver cigarette case. He lit a cigarette and stood with his back to me as he looked out the window.

'I've made arrangements,' he said—but it was a while before he turned about and looked me in the face.

'I have booked you on an afternoon flight to Geneva. From there you will take a train and cross over into France. You will reach Annecy shortly before midnight. You may take one suitcase—but only one. So, think carefully about what you want to carry.'

'How long will I be gone?'

'Who can say? A week, a month, a year—but I rather fancy you will be gone for years.'

I wanted to ask him why he was sending me away, but my throat grew tight. I threw him a pleading look.

'C'mon Harry—your mother's just died. Think carefully about what this means. She mollycoddled you—turned you soft in the head. I kicked up a fuss, but she had her way with you—and with me. Made me feel like a third class citizen, she did. Put your needs first—then came her desires. I never liked the way the two of you sat giggling together at night behind closed doors, like a couple of school girls.'

'Where are you sending me?'

'Ah yes—I should have explained. At Annecy you will be met by an old friend of mine—Father D. He is now the head of a small Catholic school for boys. He will take good care of you, Harry—far better care than I am capable of.'

Suddenly, father seemed to lose interest in the conversation. He turned away from me and took up his position by the window once again. And when I didn't move or speak, he turned around and barked, 'Go to your room and get packing.'

Shortly before midnight I arrived in Annecy. It was a chilly night but the sky was clear, and I recognized the Water-bearer perched against a tapestry of stars.

Father D had come to meet me in his black cassock. He strode up to me and studied my face. Then, taking the suitcase from out of my hand, he said, 'Come. We can walk. The school is not far from here. Besides, the best way to get to know someone is to walk with them.'

It turned out to be a long walk—and by the time we arrived I was chilled to the bone. I was led to a cell with a bunk bed, a chair and a table. Father D laid the suitcase on the bed and said, 'I'll leave you alone now: I'm sure you're tired. Breakfast will be served at seven. The showers will open at six. There's no hot water. Prayers begin at eight, followed by the first class at half past. You'll be instructed in our ways in due course. For now, I have only one question: did you bring any books?'

'Yes, Father. I brought a collection of stories by Villiers de L'Isle-Adam.'

'May I see it?'

I unfastened the leather cords around my suitcase and searched for the book. I checked to see if it had arrived without a crease—then I placed the small volume in the priest's hands. Father D inspected the book with what seemed to me exaggerated attention.

'I see you've made jottings in the margins of one of the stories. *Vera*.'

'Yes, Father.'

'This story—does it have a special significance for you?'

'My mother's name was Vera.'

'Ah, yes,'—then, handing the book back to me: 'I will allow it.'

I took the book from the priest's hands and placed it on the table. But when I turned to wish Father D good night, I found I was alone.

I have no desire to reminisce about my days at the Catholic school. From the very first, the place filled me with a sense of entrapment. The school was small and cramped and flanked by tall walls of grey-black stone. The classrooms were heaving with boys who fidgeted and looked out the window. To be sure, my French was poor and this set me apart from the other boys.

Once a week, I wrote a letter to my father. And I made a point of stacking as many details about my life at school as I could muster. But father never replied— and I began to wonder if my letters ever reached him.

I soon learned there were two kinds of boys at this school: bullies and victims. As I had never sought to dominate another human being, I soon found myself in the role of victim. Every now and then I appeared in class with a bloody nose or a cut lip; and though I nurtured dreams of revenge, I never let on to Father D how my face had been injured.

But there was one boy—nicknamed Orpheus— who was neither predator nor prey.

I remember the occasion I first set eyes on Orpheus. I had been watching my classmates playing football. There were not enough boys to make full teams, and so, two teams of five had been organized. I wanted to join in, but the boys paid me no heed: I stood by the sidelines and observed the game. At some point, I noted there were eleven boys overall. One of the teams obviously had an extra player. Then—I saw Orpheus— kicking the ball first in one direction; then passing it in another. Which team was he playing for? I glanced at the faces of the players; but no one seemed to have detected that Orpheus was playing for both sides.

Before long I wanted to become friends with Orpheus; I wanted to have his special status. In my daydreams I pictured him in his bright blue uniform; his wavy blond hair shining like a chariot in the sky; his gentle hand resting upon my shoulder. By day, we would play together on the same football team; we would pray side by side at mass. At night, we would hold clandestine meetings to discuss our innermost secrets—and I would read to Orpheus the cruel tales of Villiers de L'Isle-Adam.

Such were my fancies; but a bizarre incident put an end to these childish notions.

One day, Father D announced there would be a special mass on Wednesday. The school had its own chapel, situated underground—and we were accustomed to holding mass there on Sunday. When Wednesday came Father D led us down into the underground chapel for the extraordinary ceremony. The organ groaned in low tones and the candles flickered as if desperately holding back the darkness. We sang hymns in shrill voices and prayed on our knees. At last, Father D gave permission for us to sit.

Father D delivered a strange sermon. He told us of the demonic possession of the Ursuline nuns at Loudun in the seventeenth century and the unorthodox exorcisms of the legendary Père Surin. The quivering light of the candles caressed Father D's features. I listened to his story, entranced and captivated. My imagination now conjured up forbidden images: I saw the nuns at Loudun—their naked bodies trembling—their eyes bulging—their mouths gaping. And I saw the tall thin figure of Père Surin, praying for the salvation of their souls.

Suddenly, a deep and resonant moan, like the lowing of a cow, broke the spell. I turned about and saw Orpheus standing by my side. He was staring at me with wild eyes. Then—raising both hands to his chest, he shrieked, 'Get away from me, you devil!'—And he fell to the floor with arms thrashing.

Father D now commanded the boys to depart from the chapel. Frightened, we fought our way out of the sacred enclosure, while Father D—his body arched over Orpheus—tried to calm the boy's convulsions. As I made my exit, I turned to look at Orpheus and I saw Father D on his knees. He was thrusting the fingers of his left hand into the boy's mouth.

When I reached the surface of the earth I discovered I was shaking. I stood in the playground with my face raised to the sky, willing the sun's rays to dispel my terror. Then, I noticed there was blood on my left palm. I must have injured myself as I fled from the chapel. I made my way to the bathroom and began washing the stains off my skin.

All at once, a heavy hand descended upon my shoulder. I turned about and saw Father D.

'Follow me,' he said.

We wandered down a long hall and into a sparsely furnished room without a window. There, Father D instructed me to stand before a desk. Sitting himself opposite me, he scrutinized my face.

'The boys tell me you are a friend of Orpheus.'

Did I detect a tone of disdain?

'Orpheus is very ill,' said Father D.

'Father—is Orpheus going to die?

'Who said he was dying? He merely swallowed his tongue.'

A bewildered expression must have crossed my face, for Father D went on to explain Orpheus' condition.

'Orpheus suffered a seizure: his brain became overactive and he fell unconscious to the floor.'

'Unconscious?'

Father D nodded. 'This happens to boys who have a fertile imagination. His fantasies must have run wild.'

Then, leaning over the desk, Father D said, 'Have you been to confession lately?'

'Yes—last Sunday.'

'I'm glad to hear it. Confession is the only cure for an overactive imagination.—Is there something you want to tell me?'

'No, Father.'

'Sometimes boys talk about things they barely understand. They conjure up images in each others' imaginations and inflame their bodies unnecessarily. Do you know what I'm saying?'

'No, Father.'

Father D sighed. 'I seem to be wasting my time with you. Very well—you can go.'

'But—what will happen to Orpheus?'

'He's a sensitive boy—perhaps too sensitive for his own good. But a few days in hospital will cure him of his condition.'

Days passed and Orpheus did not return. In class, his desk stood unoccupied and forlorn. At times I would raise the lid to Orpheus' desk and look at his books and writing implements. But the days turned to weeks until, one evening, Father D cleared out Orpheus' desk.

Time ran on but I never forgot Orpheus. Indeed, I went on hoping he would come back to console me. Meanwhile, a peculiar—almost spiritual—obsession took hold of me. I felt duty-bound to Orpheus to learn as much as possible about the exorcism of the nuns at Loudun. In secret, I obtained books on the life of Père Surin—I even got hold of books written by Surin himself—and I pored over these texts as if I were reading my own destiny. One day, I acquired a series of volumes that contained Père Surin's letters. There were over four hundred letters, along with notes and commentaries; and I studied these letters for a clue to Orpheus' mysterious disappearance.

I learned from the letters that the demonic possession of the nuns had begun in 1632; but it was only in December of 1634 that Père Surin was summoned to Loudun as an exorcist. The parish priest at Loudun—Father Urbain Grandier—had been accused by the nuns of having initiated their possession. Accordingly, Father Grandier was tortured and burnt at the stake. Père Surin was then assigned to look after the spiritual health of the prioress, Jeanne des Anges. But Père Surin's method of liberating Jeanne des Anges from evil was as unexpected as it was brilliant. Rather than perform a public exorcism, he talked to Jeanne in private and behind closed doors. One by one, the demons departed from Loudun until only one demon remained—Behemoth. At last Behemoth promised to come out of Jeanne on condition that she and Père Surin made a pilgrimage to the tomb of St Francis de Sales at Annecy. And so it was that in 1638 Jeanne des Anges and Père Surin made the pilgrimage that finally liberated Loudun from the powers of evil.

Years later, and after my father's death, I had reason to remember Orpheus once again.

I had spent a sultry summer afternoon in the British Library, feeding my spiritual obsession, until at length the hour of closing arrived. I left the library in a despondent mood. The sun had not yet set and the heat was strangling my thoughts. I walked about in circles, never getting beyond the Bloomsbury area. At length I tired of wandering and the sun grew weary of shining. I entered a dimly lit public house and ordered a beer. I sat in a corner of the pub and looked about me. It was a dismal place. The lighting was weak and inadequate; the seats were plentiful but battered and old and with the smell of sweat and cigarette smoke upon them. Worse: the place was filled with old men wallowing in melancholic silence.

All at once I saw a woman sitting at the far side of the lounge. She was staring at me with large beautiful eyes, inducing a strange sense of unease in my inmost self. Although she sat unmoving I could perceive that she was unusually tall. She had long wavy reddish-brown hair; but she was pale—and I wrenched my gaze away from hers.

Suddenly, I grew hungry; I hadn't eaten all day. I called to the barman and asked if food was on hand, and I was told that there was bread and cheese and cold cuts—and nothing more. My ravenous appetite accepted this poor fare. A moment later, my dinner was placed before me. I lay the napkin on my knees and lifted fork and knife. But I was prevented from eating by a bizarre circumstance: the woman with the large eyes was now sitting at my table.

I glanced at her. I expected her to speak; but she remained silent. I looked about me; but no one seemed to notice she had joined me. I threw another glance in her direction and now saw another feature which I had overlooked. Her lower lip appeared red and swollen. I felt an uneasy mixture of attraction and repulsion.

How long we sat thus, gazing at each other I cannot remember. At length, I threw down the fork and knife and looked at the cold food before me with a sense of nausea. I glanced up into the woman's eyes and said:

'I hate this place.'

She laughed with gusto and said, 'I can see you don't belong here.'

Her comment threw me into disarray. I needed to know her name. I had to find out who I was dealing with. But before I could open my mouth, her hand shot out and she placed a finger on my lips and said:

'Don't be a fool.'

Then—she rose and looked deep into my eyes, as if pulling me with invisible strings.

'I'll wait outside,'—and she walked out of the pub.

I rose to my feet deliberately, as if I had aged. I threw down some money on the table and made my departure.

Outside, the woman was waiting for me in a black cab. The back door of the cab was flung open. I tried glancing at the driver's face, but his gaze was fixed directly in front of him. Indeed, he appeared to be as rigid as stone. I saw his hairy hands glued to the steering wheel, ugly hands with ape-like fingers. I looked about me: the street was deserted and darkness had cast its mantel on the world. I stepped into the cab and the woman gave the driver an address in Kentish Town.

The cab drove along at a leisurely pace. Every now and then the metallic light from the lampposts came streaming in, casting a silver veil over the woman's features and lending her a cat-like appearance. I cowed in the corner: I sat in awe of the woman's firm posture and her long pale legs which were stoking up my lust. Despite the mysterious circumstances, it seemed to me that my adventure of the night was nothing more than a pickup—a prelude to cheap sex. It will soon be over, I thought. When she's had her way with me, no doubt, she'll demand that I vanish from her sight.

The cab drove into a deserted little side street and halted before a dilapidated building. The woman paid the cabby. She led me down steep and winding stairs and into a basement flat. She plunged into the flat and disappeared into darkness. It was left for me to close the door and I did so with an impending sense of gloom: I felt the night closing in on me. But the door wouldn't shut. I tried to bang it tight and somehow I cut my hand. I gave a yelp, but the woman didn't say a word. I could now feel a trickle of blood on my injured hand and I flicked the light switch—but the darkness didn't budge. I tried another switch without results. I called out to the woman, begging her to turn on the lights; but silence reigned. I flapped about in the dark labyrinth, forcing down the first stings of panic that were gathering in my stomach, until at last I saw the light of a flickering candle—and it lured me to the woman's bedroom.

She had unbuttoned her dress and let it fall upon the floor. She stood before me, naked, her look trium-phant and submissive; her pale skin glowing sickly in the stray threads of candlelight hovering in the room; her ugly feet trampling the dress. There was an aura of decay about her. I saw now her thin frame, her ribs and collarbones jutting out—lending her the appear-ance of a young boy.

For a fleeting moment, the thought crossed my mind to retreat. But then, as if guided by a will more powerful than my own, I undressed and stood before her, my body shivering with cold. She shook her hair and leaned her head back—and it was the sight of her neck which stirred my lust to breaking point. I pounced on her like a starving dog: I lifted her and flung her on the bed—and I swam in her flesh until at length I sank into an exhausted sleep.

When I awoke darkness still prevailed. The cool air of night struck my naked chest. Suddenly, I felt the bed shaking. I turned and glanced at my companion of the night. One look at her bulging eyes and gaping mouth told the story. I realised at once that she was in the throes of an epileptic attack—and I drew back in horror.

Then—I seized her shoulders and shook her with a violence that surprised me.

'Wake up!' I cried.

I tried to lift her, but her thin body had gathered astounding weight, and she slipped from my hands and onto the bed. Her convulsions had gained in strength: her face was distorted beyond recognition and her fingers were curving into claws. I slapped her face—once, twice—I pulled her hair—I clutched her head with both my hands—and I shook her.

Then—from deep within my soul—a scream emerged.

'Orpheus!—Wake up!—You don't have to die, Orpheus! '

In my frantic efforts to bring the woman to consciousness, I lost my balance and we both tumbled onto the floor. All at once, I found myself under attack. She had emerged from her trance and was now battling for her freedom. Her fingers reached my face and clawed at my eyes—and I was forced to relinquish my hold. She crawled away from me and—with her back to the wall—she raised her body and stared at me in revulsion. Then—I was jolted into terror.

The woman raised her hands and covered her breasts—her mouth fell open—she gave a cavernous howl—and *I heard the voice of my father* calling to me from another world.

'Get away from me, you devil!'

ORKNEY CROSSING

I have never believed in getting on
trains, timetable in hand. I don't believe
it is in us to travel with the serenity of a
tourist, equipped for anything.

—Joseph Roth

IN the autumn of 1979 I made up my mind to visit
Scotland for no other reason than to do something
wild before I finished college. I was twenty-three and
living in a tiny room on a university campus near
London. I had just begun the final year of my psychology degree and the thought of graduating in nine
months' time filled me with sadness and dread.

I talked about Scotland with all my classmates—
and whenever I was asked why I wanted to go north,
I would give some crazy answer that satisfied no one,
not even myself.

On one occasion I said, 'I'm going to Scotland to
forget who I am.'

'In that case, I'll come with you.'

It was Arturo who spoke.

Arturo was in my class and we were friends. We had become friends early on in our acquaintance because we both felt out-of-place in England, and because we both spoke Spanish. Arturo came from Chile, but he had lived in Argentina for many years. And now, when he heard me talk about Scotland, he felt intrigued and wanted to tag along.

At first, I ignored his offer. Arturo liked to joke around, he liked to talk—and he was popular with everyone. I'd never had much use for words; I had always been quiet and morose—and the thought of spending day after day with a voracious talker filled me with disquiet.

We took the night train from King's Cross on October 17th and reached Edinburgh early next morning. It was already biting cold and we walked around looking for a cheap bed-and-breakfast. As we wandered about I became aware of the greyness of all things. Even now—as I write these lines thirty years later—even now, I cannot describe my first experience of Edinburgh in any other way than to say I was besieged by the greyness of all things. And so we found a grey hotel, situated not far from the grey train station, on a grey quiet square. The hotel room was vast, with high ceilings, and with florid wallpaper. There were two narrow creaking beds with grey bedcovers. But the price was right and the breakfast was more than any man could consume. And we roamed Edinburgh in the way tourists do, seeking out the must-see monuments and museums.

Arturo and I got along like brothers and I discovered that he too could be silent and glum. But on our fourth night occurred the incident that transformed our travel-bond.

We had gone to bed early after eating a gloomy meal in a pub. Our feet were weathered and we had nothing to talk about. It had just gone eleven o'clock when Arturo rolled over and began to snore. Even though my eyelids were heavy with gravity, I decided to read. I had brought two books with me: Neil Gunn's novel *The Snake* and Robert Louis Stevenson's *Kidnapped*. I chose *The Snake*. Soon, I dozed off and the book slipped from my grasp and thumped on the floor. I was too weary to pick it up: I turned out the light and was catapulted into a terrifying dream.

I dreamt I was standing on a beach looking at the limitless sea. And I knew that behind me stood a stranger. I dared not turn around. But I plucked up the courage to speak.

'Where am I?'

The stranger said, 'You needn't bother about that right now. The ferry will be along soon.'

'Where am I going?'

'North.'

'But why?'

'Because sooner or later everyone goes north.'

So saying, the stranger stepped closer. I could feel him wheezing on my neck. I could smell his rancid breath. Then, his hand reached over my shoulder and covered my eyes and—I awoke.

When I opened my eyes, the terror that had gripped my dream self now crossed over into consciousness. I was lying on my side. I could see Arturo's back. But my limbs were paralysed. I moved my lips but no sound emerged. And I thought: the stranger is in the room. Any moment now he'll touch me with his icy fingers.

I gave a silent scream and descended into blackness.

When I awoke next morning the light filtering through the dismal curtains filled me with despair. I had to drag my body to the breakfast room. Arturo was tucking into his fry-up, but I couldn't bear the smell of sausages or the sight of bacon. I gulped down coffee after coffee until I found the guts to speak my mind.

'We have to part,' I said.

Arturo looked hard at me.

'I mean it: we have to go our separate ways,' I insisted.

Presently, Arturo said, 'Have I offended you?'

'Look, where do you want to go next?'

'Well, if it were up to me, I'd go to the Isle of Skye.'

'That settles it. You go west—I'll go east.'

'Are you serious?'

'I'll go to Aberdeen.'

Arturo snapped, 'Is Aberdeen going to help you forget?'

We checked out of the hotel on the morning of the 22nd and made our way to the railway station. I accompanied Arturo to his train. I still had to wait for the Aberdeen express to come along from Glasgow, so I waved to my friend as his train pulled out, promising to see him in London in three days time. Then, I bought a takeaway coffee and sat and watched the indicator as it announced arrivals and departures. So there I sat, musing on the destinations that were flashed before my weary eyes. Suddenly, I saw the name Thurso—and I remembered the name because I'd seen it on the map of Scotland that I was carrying in my bag.

The Aberdeen express pulled in and I made my way to the ticket barrier. I extended my ticket to the guard, but on impulse I pulled back my hand. The guard frowned. My hand was shaking and I didn't know why. Meanwhile, passengers were rushing to board the express. But I kept thinking: Thurso—the end of the line—the northern outpost—sooner or later everyone goes north.

Then the guard broke my reverie.

'C'mon lad, the train's about to leave.'

'I'm sorry,' I said—and I marched away and boarded the train to Thurso.

No sooner had the train pulled out than I fell into a dreamless sleep. Some time later, I was wakened by stray threads of sunlight caressing my cheeks. I gazed out the window and my heart leapt with joy. At last, I had abandoned the greyness of all things. I saw the sea—the beautiful foaming sea, crashing against the shore. I saw the leaves on the trees, a kaleidoscope of colours that dazzled my eye. And I saw the sky—the benevolent sky hovering above me like a protective shield. The train was racing along the eastern coast of Scotland. Like a pair of hungry seagulls, my eyes gobbled up the landscapes as they flitted by. And in the afternoon, when the train pulled into Thurso, I stood on the beach and looked out on the waters.

I made enquiries about the ferry to Orkney and was informed that there were two hours to wait: the ferry was late on account of the high winds. I wandered about, taking pleasure in the icy bursts that were slapping my face. Then I grew hungry and I searched for a place to eat. In a colourless cafe I bought a sandwich and a bowl of soup. I sat by the window and waited for my first glimpse of the ferry. At the back of the cafe a radio was blurting out a pop song. I had finished my meal and was now ordering a cup of tea, when the pop song was cut short by a news bulletin announcing a calamity.

The Glasgow-Aberdeen express had crashed.

When I boarded the ferry to Orkney on that tragic Monday of October 22 1979, I did not, as yet, possess a detailed knowledge of the train crash. I knew only the broad outlines of my fate: the train I had intended to board earlier that morning had collided. I had escaped injury or even death—and a dream had saved me. On board the ferry, I sat in the lounge and pored over a copy of the local afternoon paper.

I read that the 08:44 passenger service from Glasgow to Dundee had been experiencing technical difficulties with its diesel locomotive earlier that morning. At approximately 10.56 it passed the Longforgan

Signal Box. Soon after, the train made a brief stop at Invergowrie station, although by now it was running twenty-five minutes late. It left Invergowrie without adequate power to continue its journey and after struggling 540 yards beyond the station, it came to a standstill.

At 11.09 the Glasgow-Aberdeen express reached the Longforgan Signal Box and proceeded to the next section where it should have come to a halt, for the signalman had indicated *Danger*. But the Aberdeen express continued on its journey. The Longforgan signalman now raised the alarm, but it was too late to prevent the catastrophe. The Aberdeen express passed through Invergowrie station at seventy miles an hour and the driver, noticing the stationary train a few hundred yards ahead, made a last-second attempt to bring the train to a stop.

It was estimated that the Aberdeen express collided with the Dundee train at 60 miles an hour, flinging the two rear coaches of the Dundee train into the Firth of Tay. Two other coaches were thrown against the sea wall. The locomotive of the Aberdeen express was severely damaged and its leading cab was crushed. The driver of the Aberdeen express, along with his assistant, died on impact. Two passengers sitting in the rearmost coach of the Dundee train were also killed. And an elderly lady received severe injuries from which she died later, bringing the death toll to five and the total number of persons injured to fifty-one.

I tore my eyes away from the newspaper and saw that the ferry had pulled out of harbour. Suddenly, in a burst of callous genius, I conceived a plan that even today—thirty years on—sends a shiver of shame down my spine.

Sooner or later, I thought, Arturo would hear the news. Assuming I had been on the Aberdeen train, he would contact my family. My mother and father, as well as my three brothers and sister, were living in London and they would all want to hear that I was safe. And it struck me that if I didn't call home, I would be presumed missing or even dead. I was a stranger to the Highlands—no one knew my identity. I was travelling without passport or identifying documents. I could be anyone. I could take on any name. I could vanish off the face of the planet and if I never returned home, I would have died to the life that I had so painstakingly created for twenty-three years. And when I realised that I had, for once in my life, the freedom of anonymity, I experienced an unspeakable thrill, the likes of which I have rarely encountered since.

I was pulled out of my deliberations by a sudden jolt of the ferry.

I looked out the window and saw that we were headed for a rough crossing. Gale force winds and violent waves were besieging our vessel and the crew were begging passengers to remain in their seats. I glanced about me and spied a woman travelling alone. I placed her age at twenty-one or twenty-two. She had long bushy light brown hair, but she was skinny and pale and her face was marred by a large mole on her lower lip. The fierce rocking of the waves was nauseating her. She cradled her head with both hands. Then she jumped to her feet and made a brave effort to reach the outer deck. But the sudden fist of a wave sent her sprawling at my feet.

I leaned over and gripped her elbow.

I raised her from the floor and—against the crew's advice—I took her out on deck. We sat on a bench and I told her that if she kept her eye on the horizon, she'd soon feel better. She shook her head but tried my suggestion all the same. After a while, she looked at me and said, 'We'd better go back.'

We gathered our bags and made our way to the ship's canteen. Sitting in a quiet corner, cradling hot cups of tea in our palms, we talked. She told me her name was Carol and she worked as a nurse back in Edinburgh. She was originally from Perth and had two brothers who had disappeared from her life after serving time in prison. Her mother had died when she was young. As for her father, he was a loud-mouthed unrepentant alcoholic. She was going to Kirkwall for a few days to stay with a girlfriend.

I told her my name was Arturo and that I was from Buenos Aires—and I studied her face to see the effect of my lie.

'So you speak Argentinian?'

'Of course,'—and I reeled off some phrases in Spanish.

Three hours later the ferry docked into Stromness and we boarded the bus to Kirkwall. En route, Carol scribbled some lines on a piece of paper. She folded the paper with exaggerated care and slipped it into my jacket.

'Kirkwall is a small place, but you can look me up.'

By the time we reached Kirkwall we were encircled by a dark drizzling mist. I asked Carol if she wanted to meet up that evening, but she just laughed and waved goodbye. I wandered about, asking the locals for directions to a cheap hotel. At length I took a room in an unofficial bed-and-breakfast run by an octogenarian widow on West Castle Street, a short stroll away from Saint Magnus Cathedral. I was offered a magnificent room with high windows that looked out onto a courtyard.

I flung my bag on the floor, sprawled on the soft bed and allowed the delicious weariness of the day to take hold of me. Then, I remembered Carol's scribbled note. I unfolded the scrap of message and was surprised to read: Eastern General Hospital, Seafield Street, Edinburgh.

I had expected Carol to provide me with her girl-friend's address in Kirkwall. Instead, she had given me what I took to be her work address in Edinburgh. Here was a mystery that I needed to unravel. Accordingly, I showered and shaved and changed into a fresh-smelling shirt. Then I went hunting for Carol. An old man bumbling along Kirkwall Harbour showed me the way to the most popular pub. I walked into the Torvhaug Inn on Bridge Street. I ordered a Jack Daniel and sat in a corner and waited. The hour had just struck eight.

Moments later, I became aware of a pasty-faced young man sitting near me. He had long black hair and a generous curly beard—and his black eyes were eagerly devouring my face.

'Visiting Orkney?' he said, as he rolled his own cigarette.

'I suppose I am,' I replied, sipping my whiskey and looking away.

'Good choice. Orkney has the richest wildlife in the British Isles, and its prehistoric monuments are the finest in the world.—And what might your name be?'

'Arturo—I'm from London.'

'Artery! That's a strange name. But then, London's a strange place. In fact, I never met a Londoner who wasn't a conniving, two-faced crook. Oh yes, I've been to London, and it's a wonder I didn't bump into the Anti-Christ himself.'

'What shall I call you?'

'My name's Bob. But my friends call me Black Bob.'

'So, shall I call you Black Bob?'

'If you want to be my friend.'

I sat with Black Bob that evening, downing Jacks and plugging him for information about the islands, keeping one eye on the clock and another on the door. But Carol did not appear. Shortly before ten thirty the landlord rang the bell for last drinks. I sprang to my feet, shook hands with Black Bob and stepped out into the crisp night air.

I was striding along a damp and narrow lane when a group of tipsy singers turned the corner and blocked my path. And when I tried to break through their ranks, I found a skinny female standing in my way. I looked up and saw—Carol.

Scarcely had Carol recognised me than she smiled and giggled and clapped her hands.

'You found me!—Come—I'll take you to my girl-friend's place.'

Carol said goodnight to the revellers. Then she led me down a labyrinth of dark streets. The light from the lamps was shimmering in the puddles; no wind; silence all around us. And soon we were climbing up steep wooden stairs. Carol pushed open a door and a blast of hot air slapped my face.

'But this is the kitchen!' I exclaimed.

'That's right: the front door leads into the kitchen. And there's an old-fashioned stove.'

A stack of dry wood was dozing in a corner. Carol took a couple of logs and stoked up a fire, and I was soon forced to take my jacket off. We sat by the stove and drank cider and spoke all kinds of delightful non-sense, until Carol's eyes took on an eerie glow.

'Would you wait while I shower?'

I nodded yes.

When I heard the burst of the shower I rose and looked about. I discovered that the flat consisted of two rooms: the large kitchen and the small bedroom. In the bedroom I found a mattress on the floor and a flimsy bedcover. In a corner: a rickety chair—but no other furniture. I walked up to the bathroom door: I could hear Carol drying her body. I stepped away from the door and re-entered the kitchen and now saw that it too was stripped down to bare essentials. I looked out the window and into the dark alley. Across the way I saw what appeared to be a cemetery.

I went back to my seat.

Carol came in barefoot, wearing a robe that reached down to her ankles. Her hair flowed languidly over her shoulders and covered her chest. In the flickering light from the stove she looked infinitely pale. She wandered about the room, casting her eyes here and there—as if she were looking for some long lost precious object—and at length she came and stood behind me.

I could smell her hair. I could feel her heat.

Suddenly, her hand reached over my shoulder and covered my eyes.

I leapt up in terror. Carol momentarily lost her balance. She dangled over the chair, but then regained her poise. Meanwhile, I had retreated to the window and was breathing in rapid shallow puffs. She stared at me, astonished, concerned, disappointed. I knew I had to say something—anything—and so I blurted:

'Where's your girlfriend?'

Barely had I uttered the words than her face took on one final transformation. She turned about and opened the stove. She reached for the poker and stabbed at the burning logs.

'I think you'd better go.'

After a pause, I nodded assent. I grabbed my jacket and departed.

My sleep that night was plagued by images of the previous day's events. In the morning, I ate breakfast without relish. And when I stepped out on the pavement, the sun hurt my eyes—as if I had become a creature of the night. I wandered without aim, but soon felt the need to talk to Carol. I knocked on her door, but there was no reply. I looked for her by the harbour, and around the Burgh. I killed time at the Orkney Museum, lingered over lunch at the Ayre Hotel—and in the afternoon I pounded again on Carol's door.

In the evening I returned to Torvhaug Inn and there found Black Bob, sitting in the same place where I had left him the day before. He motioned to me to join him.

'Artery, my friend—you seem downtrodden.'

'Don't you have anything better to do,' I said, with mounting irritation, 'than to sit in the same place day after day, drinking the same beer and smoking the same cigarette?'

'What seems to be the problem?'

'I can't find my friend.'

'Kirkwall is a small place. She's bound to turn up.'

Black Bob offered me a roll-up, which I declined. He lit up and continued.

'One of the advantages of a sedentary life is you get to observe people—you get to know what makes them tick. The way I see it, there are two kinds of mistakes that folks make. One, they hurt others. Two, they forget.'

'Hey, that's profound.'

'You can scoff at my philosophy if you like, but I'd say you're a typical case of forgetting.'

He paused. I waited for him to continue, but in the end I had to prod him.

'Go on—I'm listening.'

'I'm not implying that I know your sins. But I can guess. After all, this isn't the tourist season. Oh, we get the birdwatchers and the archaeologists. But you're probably the only real visitor to the island. And when a man comes off-season to the Orkneys, well, it's not sunshine and good food that's bringing him here. No, my friend, you came here because you're hiding.'

Defiantly: 'So, what's your advice?'

'Now that depends on what you're hiding from. If you're running from the law or an enemy, then my advice is to keep your head down. But if you're running from yourself, well, then I'd say your best bet is to turn around and look yourself in the eyes.'

Black Bob paused again, studying my face. At length, I stood up and thanked him for his lecture.

'I'm staying at Mrs McCaddy's on West Castle Street—red brick house—black door—lion-faced door knocker.'

'I know.'

At eight o'clock next morning I was woken by Mrs McCaddy.

'A young woman just phoned for you, but she didn't give her name.'

'Did she leave a message?'

'She said she'll be along at nine o'clock.'

'She's coming here?'

'That's what she said. You know, in my day girls didn't call on boys, especially not so early—'

I jumped out of bed and began to dress without bothering to wash. At the sight of my underwear Mrs McCaddy retreated to the kitchen, where she prepared black coffee and sausages. I barely had time to wolf down my sausages and gulp the coffee when I heard a honking at the door. I rushed outside and saw Carol, waiting for me in a worn out truck.

'I want to show you something—hop in.'

We drove west out of Kirkwall along the A965 until we reached Finstown, where we turned north into the A966. So far we had travelled in silence, but by the time we reached Breck of Cruan, I could no longer resist curiosity.

'Where are we going?'

Carol gave a nervous laugh and said, 'To the back of the north wind.'

We passed Hackland and Redland, pushing our way further north. At last, Carol made up her mind to speak.

'I don't recall much about my mother—but I do remember that she read to me at bedtime. Once she read me a story from a book by George McDonald, called *At the Back of the North Wind*. It's about a boy named Diamond. And Diamond is a lovely little creature who brings great joy to his parents.

'One night, as he's trying to get to sleep in the loft, he meets the North Wind as she's going on her routes—and they become friends. The North Wind takes Diamond on many adventures and she turns out to be a terrible lady. She does good things, but she does a lot of bad too. In one episode she sinks a ship.

Anyway, on one of their adventures she takes him to the country at the back of the north wind—a land without suffering or pain.

'When my mother read this story to me, I thought, yes, that's where I want to go. You see, my father would get drunk most days and he'd pick on my mother. They had terrible fights. And I would hide in my room and pray. Please, dear God, show me the way to the back of the north wind.'

'What happened to Diamond?'

'He died.'

Soon after we passed the village of Costa, a large body of peat-stained water appeared on our left.

'That's Loch of Swannay,' said Carol, '– now hold on to your seat.'

We swerved off to the right and onto a dirt road. Carol was forced to slow down. After a time, the dirt road became a bumpy no-road. We struggled a little further and came to a standstill.

We got out of the truck and Carol warned me not to wander off. I could hear the roaring of the waves and the cries of the seagulls. We came to a cliff and I knew we had reached the northern tip of Orkney Mainland.

Carol said, 'From here to the North Pole it's just water and ice.'

She walked along the edge of the cliff. Some time later we came to a jagged rock formation and Carol pointed to the beach below. We began our descent, using the jutting rocks as our ladder. The wind was smacking our limbs, but my body was warm with expectation.

When we landed on the sand Carol broke into a run and I chased after her. She was shouting, but her words were snatched by the wind.

Suddenly, she halted. I looked up.

We had come to the mouth of a cave. My mind now began to race ahead with questions, but Carol walked away from me. Approaching the entrance, she reached into her jacket and pulled out a torch. Throwing a brief glance in my direction, she stepped into the cave and vanished. I was suddenly assailed by a feeling of foreboding. But when I entered the cave I saw Carol casting the light in all directions and I was awed by the beautiful immensity of the secret chamber.

We pushed deeper into the cave until Carol came to a sudden halt.

'Is this the end?' I said.

'No: the cave goes on, but this is far enough,'—and she switched off the torch.

I expected my eyes to get used to the dark. But the blackness that engulfed us was complete.

'Carol?'

I could hear her moving, but I couldn't work out in which direction.

'Carol—where are you?'

'Black Bob warned me about you. At first I thought he was jealous. But I've known Bob since I was a little girl. And I've never known him to lie.'

'OK—I admit: I lied to you. My name is not Arturo.'

'And they don't speak Argentinian in Buenos Aires?'

'They speak Spanish.'

She moved again and I felt a knot in the pit of stomach.

'Carol—put the light on!'

'No—you're in the belly of the dragon. If you want your little adventure to end happily, you'll have to kill the dragon and find your way out.'

The tone of her voice was playful and menacing in equal measure. Before I could say another word, I heard the sound of shuffling feet.

Carol had departed.

I stood in the dark, uncomprehending. Then, I took two steps and was surprised to find my shoe in a puddle of water. Surprise was soon replaced by apprehension, for it was clear that I had already lost my bearings.

I took another path and stumbled into water—on this occasion the tarn reached half-way up my shin. I fought the rising tide of panic. I stretched out my arms in all directions, trying to build a mental image of my surroundings. I touched the walls of rock that impeded my path, as if interrogating their right to hold me prisoner. I crouched on the ground and felt sand and pebbles. I twirled about, looking for that faint clue of light that indicated the way out.

I had been stumbling about in the dark for some minutes, when I tripped and tumbled on my face. I felt a sharp pain in my leg. I sat up and reached for the injured area and found a gash in my jeans. Strangely, the pain that was now throbbing in my leg lulled me into stillness.

Then I gave a frightful laugh.

If I couldn't find my way out, would Carol abandon me to eternal darkness? Had I escaped death at Invergowrie only to find it in the belly of the Orkney dragon? I was amused by my predicament and I chuckled to myself. But when the joke had passed, I staggered to my feet.

When I emerged from the cave, I estimated I had been gone a mere twenty minutes and had probably explored only a hundred yards of darkness. But the timepiece in my heart told me I had aged.

I looked up at the clear blue sky. Like a convict just released from prison, I stood on the shore and offered my cheeks to the wind. But when I stumbled about on the beach I found no sign of Carol.

I climbed the rocky ladder to the top of the cliff. The truck had vanished.

It was another hour before I reached the A966. By now the sun had turned red and giant—and a thin blanket of drizzling rain was embracing the land. I hitched a lift from a grey-haired farmer riding an old Ford. We rode in silence, with the wipers whooshing monotonously all the way. By the time we made Kirkwall Harbour the night was inky black. The driver turned on the radio and I heard the Moody Blues singing *Nights in White Satin*.

My first impulse on reaching Kirkwall was to go to the Torvhaug Inn. I wanted to talk to Black Bob. But when I got there, I couldn't muster the courage to enter. Bob was right: I had come to Orkney to hide. I had taken a false name and given devious information—all in the spirit of adventure. En route I had met Carol—a kindred soul—a fellow pilgrim in search of anonymity—and I had lied to her too. Suddenly I felt lonesome and forlorn. I stood by the entrance of the inn and watched as others went in to enjoy the company of friends.

I turned my back on the Torvhaug Inn and made my way to Mrs McCaddy's, where I nursed my wounds in a steaming hot bath with smelling salts. Out of the blue I remembered Arturo. I closed my eyes, took a deep breath and sank my head under water. A minute later, I came out gasping. And I made up my mind to leave Orkney next morning, and head for the Isle of Skye.

Shortly before midnight I closed my eyes and waited for sleep. All of a sudden, I leapt out of bed and searched my jacket for Carol's note. And I deliberated one last time whether to seek her out in Edinburgh. Bit by bit, I crumpled the note with the tips of my fingers. I opened the window and flung Carol's mystery into the courtyard. I stood by the window and peered into darkness, relishing the cool stabs of the late October night.

Then I closed the window with an insolent clatter.

MEYRINK'S GAMBIT

I

IT was a mild autumn evening in 1913 and I had been out for a leisurely walk with my good friend Gustav Meyrink. We had been sauntering along the Währingerstrasse and made our way to our favourite coffee house. Selecting a table on the terrace of the Café Landtmann, we squandered the remainder of the evening on black coffees, cigars and passionate discussions of alchemy, Egyptian history and the dubious health benefits of living in an amoral city such as Vienna. At length we grew tired and I indicated to the waiter that I wished to pay.

'I'm sorry, sir,' the waiter said, 'but your bill has been settled.'

'How did that happen?' I asked.

Pointing to a vacant table that looked out onto the Rathaus, the waiter said, 'The gentleman who was sitting over there a moment ago—he paid.'

Meyrink smiled. 'Did he know us?'

'No, sir.'

'Did he pay on a whim?' I said.

The waiter's tone was apologetic. 'It was an over-sight. He paid for his drinks, sat there for a moment and then asked for his bill again. He must have forgotten that he had paid. I too forgot and by mistake I passed him your bill.'

Meyrink roared with laughter.

We thanked the waiter and sat chuckling in the evening shadows.

Presently, Meyrink said, 'Long ago I learned that chance rules our lives, often for the worse. But this was a pleasant surprise.'

'Chance? You've always asserted that our lives are guided by powerful forces outside our awareness.'

'And one of these forces is chance. Listen—I once believed that the Habsburgs would endure for-ever. But now, there is unrest in Serbia, Galicia, and Montenegro. The empire is being torn apart by its many ethnic groups and the economy suffers. Our industries are losing business to foreign competitors. The metal industry is on the decline; the cotton mills are closing down. The slums continue to expand like mushrooms. And last year fifteen hundred Viennese tried to take their lives. Fifteen hundred! As for the Emperor—he's a very old man.'

'There *is* a successor,' I offered.

'A successor,' echoed Meyrink, 'but for how long? Oh, let's not deceive ourselves: the end is near. The question is: who will strike the fatal blow? I predict that a chance event will end our world. Somewhere, some small act by an unknown individual will bring

Europe to its knees. You don't believe me? Well, let me tell you a story that will convince you.'

The hour was late and I craved sleep, but I knew that Gustav was about to paint one of his profound insights into the human condition. So I lit another cigar, leaned back in my chair and listened to his tale.

II

One afternoon of a Sunday in August of this year, I had been strolling along the Graben when I suddenly changed direction and headed towards the Burggarten. I crossed the park, came out onto the Ring and continued my stride until I saw the green copper dome of the Karlskirche. I scanned the Karlsplatz and there saw, at the corner of a lonely street, a café with a strange name—The Museum.

The late summer sun pressed harsh on my face. Accordingly, I entered the Museum. I approached the woman behind the counter, ordered a Hennessy, and looked around for a place to sit. I settled into one of the alcoves, cognac in hand, and my eyes wandered around the interior of the café. The walls were grey and bare, and a melancholic—almost ascetic—atmosphere lingered about the place. Old men pored over newspapers, smoke filled the air; it was the kind of place where loners, who wanted to remain anonymous, could hide.

All at once I spied a group of chess players at the far end of the café. They had gathered around a chessboard, playing winner-stays-on, and the sight of the chess pieces took me back to my childhood in Munich and the memory of my mother Maria Wilhelmina. On my fourth birthday she taught me to play chess—the Game of Kings as she called it—and within a handful of years I became a strong devotee of the game who could hold his own against the best players in the city. But I had not played in many years, and now, as I gazed upon the chess enthusiasts standing around the board, I felt drawn to the game once again.

I leapt to my feet and glided towards the players.

One glance at the chessboard sufficed to ascertain that White was going to win. It was Black's move: I saw at once the imperative need to regroup his minor pieces. True, Black would lose in the end, but a stubborn defence would delay defeat. To my disappointment, Black played weakly and the game came to a premature end.

'You should have centralised your pieces,' I exclaimed.

The chess players turned to look at to me, amazed.

'No need to be surprised, gentlemen,' I said, 'there was no other way to prolong the defence.'

'I believe you're right,' said White. 'Would you care for a game?'

A game of chess! Years had passed since my last game, but I was confident that my chess skills had not deteriorated. The few moves of the game that I had witnessed convinced me that it would not be difficult to defeat them all.

I took my place at the chessboard and positioned the pieces onto their original squares. As I did so, I studied my opponent out of the corner of one eye. He was a small man, with lanky brown hair and pale skin, of about forty years. His gestures were graceful and elegant and an aura of strength and vulnerability hovered about him. He wore a white cotton suit that had seen better days.

The chess set ready, the time had come for the introductions.

'I am Kubin,' my opponent began, 'Alfred Leopold Kubin—artist.'

I gave Herr Kubin a courteous bow and said, 'Meyrink. Gustav Meyrink—I am a connoisseur of strange and forgotten things.'

'I have read your stories, and they are certainly strange. But please, would you care to play white? I hope you won't be offended, but it is a tradition in this café that a new player moves first.'

I opened the game by advancing the king's pawn two squares, letting my opponent know that I favoured a game of open combat. I had never developed the sly, devious methods of some chess players, who manoeuvre their pieces behind the pawns. Attack, sacrifice and storming the castled position—these were my methods. After half a dozen opening moves, I played my gambit: I sacrificed my king's knight, forcing my opponent's king into the centre. My minor pieces took control of the central squares. I castled. I probed my opponent's position with my queen. I doubled my rooks. I embarked on a wild attack that risked all. To my delight, I saw Kubin dig into his position, seeking to block my pieces with his pawns. All at once it all came back to me: the delirious pleasure of attacking a player whose pieces were uncoordinated. In my youth, I had played many similar games and revelled in the excitement that comes from crushing one's opponent. I was convinced that victory would be mine. I felt twenty years younger. Blood pounded in my forehead.

I ordered another Hennessy while Kubin plunged deep into thought. The waiter brought my drink on a silver tray. I gulped the cognac down and waited for my opponent's resignation.

At last, Kubin made his move, thrusting a pawn against my castled king. I was forced to capture the pawn, but I did so with confidence in my game. Then—the surprise. When I least expected it, when victory seemed within my grasp, at the height of my sadistic pleasure in my opponent's cramped position, Kubin made a move that threw me: he sacrificed his knight. It was an astounding defence, all the more so as his move seemed like a mirror reflection of my own attack. I knew at a glance that my opponent had escaped defeat and I expected the game to flow quietly into a draw. But no! He began stabbing my position with his pawns, first in the centre, then on the flanks. My king's sanctuary was torn open and I made a wild bid to save the game by running my king from one side of the board to another. But my opponent's heavy pieces hounded the white monarch until at last he found peace at the edge of the board.

Checkmate.

The silence in the grey café roared in my ears; no one stirred. I stared at the board in disbelief, like an old man who wakes up one morning to discover that life has passed him by. Then, I heard Kubin's faraway voice.

'A brilliant attack, Herr Meyrink—a pity you could not win.'

After the game, my opponent invited me to a glass of Hennessy in a quiet alcove by a window. No sooner had we settled in our seats than I asked Herr Kubin for his opinion on our game.

'Where did I go wrong?'

Kubin shrugged his shoulders. 'Perhaps you were just unlucky.'

'Your knight sacrifice—'

'It was a random move in a desperate position.'

I laughed, 'It's kind of you to say so, Herr Kubin, but chess is a game of skill and logic.'

'I think, my friend, that you underestimate the all-pervasive nature of chance. Has it ever occurred to you that in the course of one's lifetime, one is granted certain opportunities and not others?'

'Of course—but chess is not life.'

'It is better than life! Whoever invented the game was a genius. It is the closest we have come to creating a perfect world. But even in chess we find the mysterious workings of chance.'

'Ah, Herr Kubin, I must disagree with you. The game of chess is a reflection of the human mind, and the mind works according to certain immutable laws.'

'Such as?'

'Such as love and death,' I said. 'Our lives are governed by an endless search for an ideal love and an unquenchable longing for death.'

A long pause followed. I heard the clinking of glasses as the waiter cleared a table. Night had fallen. Through the window I saw a carriage pass by, its dim lamp sputtering. Kubin lit a cigar and ordered another round of drinks.

'Once upon a time I might have agreed with you,' Kubin resumed. 'You see, as a young man, my ambition was to become a priest.'

'A priest!'

Kubin brushed the newly fallen ashes off his jacket. 'That surprises you? As a collector of forgotten things, you must have come across some strange confessions. Very well, I will tell you the story of my youth. Who knows? You might use it one day.'

Kubin paused and looked at his cigar. He sipped his cognac and then began.

III

'My father was a lame wolf. At least, that's how I imagined him all through my childhood. I was afraid of his bite. I marvelled at his stern voice and passion for order. He was as old-fashioned as a Pharaoh's tomb. But I believed—or wanted to believe—that a weakness could be found in his armour. His eyes were inexhaustibly dark; his eyebrows protruded like knives from his forehead; his hands were rugged and twisted. But in my daydreams, his body took on a thin and brittle shape, like a dry old twig that snaps under one's foot.

'I grew up in Bohemia, in Litoměřice, and from a young age I proved to be a delicate and oversensitive creature. My mother was a talented pianist, but when she died—I was only ten—I told my father that I wanted to enter the priesthood; that I felt called from Another World; and I wanted my religious education to begin at once. A year later my father remarried and my stepmother—a devout woman with a passion for Bach—became enraptured by my wish to become a servant of God. But father rarely heeded her wishes. He would say that she was not the kind of woman one reads from cover to cover, and only the heavens knew why he had married her. She was attractive, yes, with vibrant young eyes and delicate hands, but my father perused her only occasionally.

'I always felt there were dark notes to my stepmother that my father did not know how to play, that behind her clear and simple manners there echoed deep melodies, hidden passions, resounding desires, and that these incomprehensible strivings had had to be channelled into music and her prayer book. A year after my mother's death, my stepmother also left this earth and I was apprenticed to Alois Beer, the landscape photographer. The years trickled by. But my mind was on the Other Side, and in time my father grew tired of my priestly ambitions.

'One day, he informed me that he had made arrangements for my future. I was to be enrolled in the Special Cadet Corps at Pest. The old wolf had mapped out my life and I dared not, at that young age, defy him.

'I entered the military Academy in 1896. I was nineteen, and from the first day I disliked everything and everyone around me. The regimented life was not for me and it seemed that my fellow cadets were little better than animals. They were intellectually shallow, commonplace and vulgar. There were endless demands to conform to this and that rule, and the upshot of it all was that I became a violent individualist, a silent rebel against all ties and constraints. The boys at the Academy came to hate me, called me all manner of names: a weakling, a snob, a poor sport. And the more they hated me, the stronger my individualism, the more I thirsted for freedom.

'One morning, our commanding officer—the ever-irritable Captain Pázmány—announced that in place of lessons we would go swimming, and I, who did not know how to swim and was too proud to admit it, became panicky. We were taken to a quiet spot on the Danube and allowed to swim freely, to play and enjoy ourselves. For once, Captain Pázmány did not bark orders. He remained content to watch the cadets as they strolled along the river, conversing and laughing. But I could not join in, my thoughts were focused on one thing only: how to make the officer and cadets believe that I could swim?

'A chance event came to my rescue. Two boys who had been disputing God only knew what became embroiled in an argument with fists. All attention became concentrated on the boys; our commander called out to them to cease fighting. I grasped that moment as a dying man claws for one last breath. I stole away

130

unseen and found a secluded spot along the Danube where no one could spy on me. I waded in the shallow waters of the magnificent river—making sure to wet my hair—and then returned to the fold. I walked as close to the commanding officer as I dared. I wanted him to see the water dripping off my body and almost as soon as I had reappeared, I began to shiver from the cold.

'The Captain saw me and called out, "Kubin! You've done enough swimming for today. Dry yourself and get dressed."

'That evening, as the lights in our sleeping hall were extinguished, I lay in bed silently gloating over my triumphant act of deception. I had fooled them all, and it had all been so simple and without effort. They were idiots, each and every one of them, and the commanding officer was the greatest idiot of them all. But my victory was short-lived, for a few days later Captain Pázmány announced that we would be returning to the river, only this time the cadets would be tested. There was to be a swimming competition with prizes and special privileges for the best swimmers. I should have gone straight to the Captain and admitted my weakness. But pride—that lascivious angel—pounded in my veins. I will learn to swim, I thought, in secret and in haste.

'In the main building of the Academy, at the end of a long and desolate corridor, there was a swimming pool that had not been used in months. One afternoon, I slithered away unseen with the intention of practising my strokes. But the door was locked and I realised that I would have to borrow the key from the concierge—but without his knowledge.

'Later that night, as my fellow cadets lay buried in their dreams, I threw back my bedcovers, fled the sleeping hall unseen, crossed the courtyard, and entered the main building. The concierge was not in his office. Most likely, he would be prowling around, checking doors and windows. I slipped into his office, took the key to the pool from its ledger and made my way down the grim corridor where clear waters lay waiting to ambush me.

'Inside the long swimming hall darkness throbbed. But a full moon shone through the windows and I saw no reason to light the lamp. I pondered whether I should lock myself in, but even if my absence were noted, who would think of looking for me in the pool in the blackness of night?

'I undressed and stood by the shallow edge of the pool. I had heard that one could teach oneself to swim. But was it possible that there were rare individuals who did not need to learn, who had the knowledge already in their bones and in their muscles? Perhaps I was one of those rare persons. Perhaps if I dived in I would come up triumphant, a natural swimmer. The longer I stood there, the greater my conviction that I had only to dive in and all would be well. At length I walked around to the deep end, stood solemnly at the edge and thought: once again I will fool them all. When my fellow cadets next see me, they will be gazing at a competent swimmer. Who knows? I might even win the swimming prize.

'I stepped out into the air and sank feet first into the water, confident that I would be buoyed up to the surface. But I continued to sink and to my surprise, I felt my feet touch the bottom of the pool. For a brief moment, the serpent of fear gripped my heart. But I took control of my reflexes. I leapt up and thrashed about as if trying to crawl my way out of a deep hole. A moment later, my head emerged on the surface. I gulped air and at once began my slow descent to the bottom. I cannot remember how many times I repeated the manoeuvre. But I do remember that as my strength gave out, a fear took hold of me—the terror of non-existence. In the end, my stamina collapsed and there came the dreadful realisation that I had muscle to make one, and only one, last desperate leap.

'When my head pierced the surface of the water, I filled my lungs with air, as if hoarding precious stones for a long journey into an unknown land. Suddenly, I glimpsed a moving shadow: someone had entered the swimming hall. But I had started my final descent into the dark waters and I had not the strength to call out. I felt the liquid embrace dragging me down into blackness, and with the last grain of desire for life I lifted my arm out of the water.

'Then came the incident that has haunted me ever since. As my feet touched bottom and death's dark glove began to fold around me, I saw my father at the bottom of the pool, standing proud and menacing. All at once his eyes took on a fearful shine. He looked up and began to swim away to safety. And I, in my terror of the dark waters, I held on to him, pulled him down, clawed at him to remain with me in this kingdom of no return. He fought me. He struggled to be free of my embrace and our limbs, the fleshly carriers of infinite horror, became entangled. At last, my lungs gave out and water worked its way into my being.

'When I next opened my eyes, I was lying on a soft bed and could not at first understand how I had got there. Certainly, I was surprised to discover that I was still alive. Standing around the bed were two men, one dressed in white, the other in army uniform. I glanced around me and studied the scant objects in the room.

'All at once, I knew: I was in the army hospital.

'It all came back to me: the key, the pool, the concierge and my unhappy attempt to teach myself to swim in the darkness of night. The man in white—a nurse—now whispered in my ear. I could not at first understand his words, but from his tone of voice I detected his concern. I must have brushed shoulders with Death; I must have been unconscious when the concierge dragged me out of the water. I turned my gaze onto the uniformed man and recognized him as my commanding officer—and my childish dreams of deceiving my peers fell to ruins.'

Kubin paused. His face had taken on a strained appearance, as if he were struggling with an unmentionable idea. He looked hard at me and went on.

'I expected to be punished. I awaited my humiliation or even expulsion from the Academy. But a strange coincidence came to my rescue and my faux pas was soon forgiven. I was given an honourable discharge: my father had collapsed and was in coma. But most uncanny of all was that he had lost consciousness on the night that I had nearly drowned. He had stopped breathing, suddenly, and without warning.'

Kubin's cigar had cooled. Our glasses were empty. The waiter was arranging the chairs in quartets on the wooden tables.

'It was rumoured later that I had attempted suicide,' said Kubin, 'and that I had had to leave the military on account of a nervous breakdown. What happened at the bottom of that pool—who can say? I knew that I was alive, not because of divine intervention or destiny, but merely because I had not—by chance—turned the key in the lock. My father survived his collapse and struggled on in ill health for a few more years. But after the incident in the pool I renounced my desire to serve God and gave myself entirely to the artistic life—as my mother would have wanted. I studied painting under the gentle guiding hand of Ludwig Schmitt-Reutte. Later, I enrolled at the Munich Academy, where I discovered the awesome prints of Max Klinger and Francisco Goya. And in time I became the self-absorbed and solitary artist that I am today.'

The gaslights were fluttering away one by one. The waiter brought our bill and Kubin waved to me that he would pay.

'So you see, Herr Meyrink, how chance rules our lives.'

Scarcely had Meyrink concluded his extraordinary tale than we left Café Landtmann and wandered along the Ring. He accompanied me as far as the Heidenplatz before bidding me goodnight. As I made my way home, I pondered his story, but I dared not accept the premise that our lives are guided by accident and co-incidence. Chess as a game of chance—a preposterous idea! And Gustav's claim that a random knight sacri-fice had brought down his carefully constructed attack seemed equally absurd.

Eight months later, I had cause to remember Meyrink's prophecy.

On the morning of June 28, 1914, our world was brought to ruins: Archduke Franz Ferdinand, the successor to the throne, and his wife Sophie, were assassinated at Sarajevo.

Early that morning the Archduke's motorcade had set out along the Appel Quay, when, shortly after ten o'clock, an explosion shook the city. A bomb destined for the Archduke's car had been thrown wide of its mark and the Archduke remained unharmed. Some crowds scattered, others pushed their way closer to the Archduke's vehicle. Police swarmed about like frenzied bees until at length they gave the order to evacuate the devastated area.

Police now gave instructions to the chauffeur of the lead car: he was to drive his vehicle—brimming with government agents—in the direction of the garrison hospital. But the driver made a wrong turn along the

Appel Quay, leading the motorcade into a side street. General Potiorek, seated in the front of the second car, noticed the mistake and called out to the lead car to turn back. Obeying these new orders, the chauffeur in the lead car stopped and prepared to make a U-turn. But as the lead car came to a halt, and with it all of the motorcade, the Archduke's car came to rest but five feet from a tall, frail youth with eyes the colour of the limitless sky.

It was Gavrilo Princip, the commander of the mission to assassinate Franz Ferdinand.

Archduke and assassin gazed at each other with fascinated eyes. Then—in a gesture both elegant and swift—Princip removed the Browning from his jacket and aimed at the Archduke. The sight of the Duchess momentarily disconcerted him and he looked away before firing twice. Blood trickled down the Duchess' silk white dress, staining her bouquet of white roses. The Archduke's mouth vomited red. Then, in a moment of insight, before death overtook him, the Archduke said, 'Little Sophie, little Sophie, don't die! Stay alive for the children!'

But little Sophie had slumped against his shoulder, and even as the car sped away from the centre of violence, by the time the church bells of Sarajevo rang eleven o'clock, the Archduke and his Sophie lay eternally still.

DOÑA ARIANA'S GLASS FOOT

WHEN I stroll through the city my eyes trail the ground, hunching my tall thin frame into a question mark, and if I wear a hat or a raincoat, I could be mistaken for a middle-aged man. But if you heard my high-pitched voice or shook my pale glossy hands, you would know at once that I was young and inexperienced. I confess: it has not been long since I left school and to this day I am haunted by the memory of my classmates whispering in the shadows, trading stories of their pretended sexual exploits. Such talk has always fascinated me; women have always fascinated me; I have always been afraid of women. And so it was with some trepidation that I accepted my sister Bianca's invitation to a tea party at her mansion in San Francisco, where, she assured me, I would be introduced to *a certain lady*.

I arrived at Bianca's tea party on the appointed day, the day before my university entrance examinations, a beautiful summer's day graced by acrobatic swallows and the smell of ocean salt. I found my sister standing by the high iron gates, quivering with impatience and the usual shame. Yes, shame, for although my sister's facial features were much like my own, she felt ashamed of the freckles that smeared her arms and shoulders like a galaxy of dark stars, and she had never understood how I, who had been born without physical imperfections, had remained unmarried.

I kissed her on the cheek and uttered the usual lie.

'Hello sister, you look pretty as always.'

'Hello Vincent,' she replied, 'it's good of you to come. You look attractive in your white cotton suit. How are your studies progressing?'

We chatted in an animated fashion about the most insignificant things, and at length she led me down the corridors of her grand and imposing house and into the garden where the guests had gathered. There were couples old and young savouring deep-red wines. Servants dressed in white gloves and black bowties served costly delicacies on silver platters. My nose itched at the smell of burning rum, Havana cigars and roasted coffees. My ears buzzed with the monotony of the gossiping voices, and behind the voices—the faint echo of a piano.

But I was bored.

I forgot the names of the guests and made ready to depart. It was at the moment when I prepared to flee, when I looked at my watch and feigned a hurried look—it was at that moment that Bianca carried out her plan of introducing me to *a certain lady*.

On previous occasions my sister had introduced me to rich, young women of my own age. Doña Ariana, however, was beautiful. Spellbound, I gazed upon her ravaged face and corrupt mouth, her alluring grey-blue eyes and thick white hair. She moved towards me with slow, graceful steps; offered me her hand and spoke to me in a rich voice that seemed to come from deep within the earth. I knew not what to say or what to do. Like a tree turned to stone, I had lost the power to move of my own accord; a force more savage than my will drew me towards this magnificent lady.

At last, I edged towards her, intending to shake her hand, but the entire weight of my huge body, concentrated in my right leather shoe, came down on Doña Ariana's pale and delicate left foot; a foot that perched on the flimsiest high heels that I had ever seen.

'You clumsy, stupid man!' she howled.

I had made a fool of myself. I had hurt the woman that my sister had brought to my attention. I had indeed acted the part of a clumsy, stupid man. The upshot of it all was that my soul plunged into guilt and to atone for my sin, I remained at the party and gave all my time to the injured lady.

We sat in a far corner of the garden, where old chestnuts shaded us from darting eyes and stray ears. I ordered extravagant delicacies and old wines to be brought to our table. I made every effort to entertain Doña Ariana: I talked without pause; I confessed my most secret desires, my burning ambitions. I revealed to the old woman my dream of becoming a world famous archaeologist. Silent, she sat in the shade of the chestnuts, her ears clinging to my words, her eyes boring through my skin.

The church bells were ringing the midnight hour when I returned to my apartment, and almost as soon as I had entered, I realised that guilt—that old bloodhound—had followed me home. I felt that my debt to Doña Ariana had not been paid: I would have to see her again. In the night, I dreamt that I held the old woman's foot in my right hand, but that the foot turned to glass, slipped from my grip, fell, and shattered on the hard polished floor of my apartment.

Early next morning, I forgot my university examinations. The calling of her flesh to the animal within me swept aside all my earthly ambitions, and I raced to Doña Ariana's house, situated in a dreary corner of Dolores Street. The image of her delicate foot aroused me to fantastic dreams of brutal possession in which she, the cautious and refined jewel, surrendered to my every whim.

But I was no longer the master of my dreams: Doña Ariana's lovemaking made me forget that she was forty years my senior.

My desire for her became unquenchable. We thrashed about in her narrow bedroom like freshly caught eels. But the more I squandered my body, the deeper my guilt. In time, I squandered everything: my apartment, my savings, the trust fund bequeathed to me by my belated father—all were signed over to Doña Ariana. A spider of infinite greed, she feasted on all that I had. Homeless, penniless, I witnessed my archaeological future crumbling into ruins, all on account of my guilt.

When Bianca heard of my shame, she searched for me in the deserted streets along the harbour. One night, down a narrow lane, she found me sleeping on the pavement. I was wrapped in rags that clung to my body like discarded strips of bacon. My eyes were frozen and my speech had the flavour of madness. That same night, she took me into her home, fed me, clothed me, brought me back to life, and together, we plotted revenge under the low stars and the spitting rain.

A month after my sister rescued me from the streets we murdered Doña Ariana in her home. Under cover of darkness of a new moon, we rang her bell and waited for the old spider to let us into her dominion. We heard her cautious footsteps as she approached the door, but it was only after I had called out to her, sang her name and begged her to let me in, that we heard the bolts slide and the door open. When she saw that I had come with Bianca, she made to shut us out, but together we forced our way in, threw the old woman to the floor, shouting grotesque names in her ear. The old spider fought back and we were astounded by her strength and will to live.

She ran to the window that looked on to the square, broke the glass with her bare hands and screamed, called for help, squealed like a pig at the moment of slaughter. I pulled her away from the window and flung her across the room, and as she fell, I saw her foot, the source of my guilt and weakness.

Paralysed as I was by the sight of her white, fragile foot, it fell to Bianca to carry out the foul deed, strangling the old woman with a piece of string. I watched in horror and fascination as life flowed out of Doña Ariana's beautiful-cruel eyes, her arms outstretched in my direction, her body writhing and contorting, silently pleading for help, begging for one last gasp.

After a long struggle, life took its leave of the old woman. Protected by the extraordinary darkness, we carried her body to the harbour, lowered it into the waters, pinning our hopes on the slow, watery powers of the Pacific to bring decay and dissolution to all things.

Our revenge fulfilled, I thought then that my life would begin to flow along the old channels. I would return to my studies, regain my ambitions and Bianca would continue to give lavish parties where I would be introduced to young women of wealth, if not beauty. But days after we had disposed of the old woman, I read in the San Francisco Chronicle that Doña Ariana's body had been found, washed ashore on a beach. Rats had gnawed at her eyes and skin, but police had identified her after neighbours had reported her disappearance. I had always considered Doña Ariana as a solitary—a person without friends and family. But there were those who mourned her and an extravagant funeral was arranged by the citizens of the city, a funeral that was attended by hundreds of men and women—mostly men—and included important political figures and members of State.

When I discovered that others had loved Doña Ariana, I found that my guilt had not been appeased. I felt haunted by the memory of my faux pas. The image of her suffering foot burned in my mind. I realised to my horror: I still desired her.

'You are not the first man to be consumed by guilt,' Bianca admonished me one day.

'Is there no way to escape my inner turmoil?' I asked.

'My dear Vincent, you must marry. Many are those who are besieged by passion. You must find a woman who will embody all that you desire.'

'But I still long for Doña –'

'Come, let us not talk about this any more,' she interrupted. 'I will arrange a new tea party to take place at the next full moon. You must attend this party, dear brother, and there, I shall introduce you to *a certain lady*.'

I trembled at my sister's words. Did she truly believe that after having been an accomplice to murder, that after my cowardly actions, I could still find a respectable position in society?

The days slipped by and the full moon tumbled into my room. I made ready for Bianca's tea party as if preparing for the guillotine. I washed and shaved twice. I shaved first using my usual method and then a second time against the grain. I studied my tired face in the mirror, put on a fresh, white shirt and dazzling white tie, inserted the silver cuff-links that had once belonged to my father, and put on a dark-blue dinner jacket that I had brought back from the Dominican Republic some years before. From my bedroom on the top floor of the mansion, I could hear the voices of the guests as they arrived: the time had come to descend into the meaningless chatter that accompanies social events.

I straightened my tie and buttoned my jacket. I lit a cigar and looked out the window at the blue-black ocean.

I finished my cigar, threw the butt-end out the window, left the bedroom and descended the stairs that led to the large hall where the guests were gathered, and where Bianca hoped to seal my future. But when I reached the entrance to the party, I froze—I listened to the gay voices that teased my ears and were fast becoming abhorrent to me with every passing moment. I cannot remember how long I stood there, nor can I recall the dark thoughts that passed through the grim alleys of my imagination, but at length, I pulled away from the door, returned to the stairway and descended to the basement, where Bianca kept all manner of forgotten objects, spare furniture, tools and old wines. I stumbled around in the dim light until I found what I was looking for: a crowbar, a shovel and a small axe. I placed the tools in a small canvas bag, slung the bag over my shoulder, retraced my steps and abandoned the house with its vile guests.

A cool rain began to fall as I entered the Mission Dolores Church Cemetery. I had gathered from the newspapers that Doña Ariana had been buried in an obscure area somewhere along the wall on Sixteenth Street. I stumbled about in the dark, reading the inscriptions on the tombstones, feeling myself grow heavy as the rain soaked my elegant attire. It was if the rain were intent on pushing me into the ground, trying to unite me with the last remnants of my deepest desire.

At length, I found her gravestone and I was astonished at the simplicity of the inscription. It read—

Here Lies a Certain Lady

I lost no time in carrying out the grim act that my guilt compelled me to perform. I took the shovel from the bag and began to dig. Raindrops lashed the earth, transforming the ground into a slimy brown mass that seemed to suck me deeper into my ultimate destination. An hour passed, two, three! How deep would I have to dig to find the old lady who had taken all that I possessed and was even now calling me from another world, asking for more?

Suddenly, the shovel met with resistance. Before long I had dug up Doña Ariana's coffin, forced open its lid with the crowbar, and there found the last shreds of decaying flesh and bone that had once had the power to bring a man to his doom.

Some magic still remained in the old spider: I dropped to my knees and wept.

My guilt had brought me thus far and as I wept among the ruins of my passion, I knew that guilt would guide me through the last stretch of my lonely journey. There was one final act to perform, the only one that might release me from the debt that I still owed to Doña Ariana's damaged foot. With my bare hands I plucked the old woman's remains out of the coffin and threw the old bones onto the wet earth. I took the axe out of the bag, raised it with both hands above my head, and, imbuing the axe with the entire weight of my enormous body, I brought the axe down and severed Doña Ariana's left foot from the remains of her body. I dropped the axe, picked up the muddy foot and slipped it into the inner pocket of my dinner jacket. Without bothering to collect my tools or return the remnants of Doña Ariana to their resting place, I abandoned the cemetery and retraced my steps in the direction of Bianca's full-moon party, where *certain ladies* dressed in magnificent outfits awaited my return.

A MASTER CLASS WITH JOSEPH ROTH

Napoli, 29 November 1999

GRANDPA died early this morning. How long I sat by the side of his bed, cradling his head in my arms, I cannot remember. In the end, I took his withered hands and laid them on his chest. But I could not bring myself to close his eyes. Then I went and locked myself in the study.

30 November, morning

I am sitting in the study at grandpa's desk, putting my thoughts down on paper. Now that he is dead I feel an unaccountable impulse to write. Did I sleep yesterday? I believe I did. But I spent most of my waking hours reliving my grandfather's ultimate moments.

I had heard grandpa coughing in the night, cursing, tossing and turning—then I heard him call my name, and I shuffled along in my slippers, down the long hall of the decrepit house.

'I'm afraid to leave you empty-handed,' he said to me as soon as I had entered—and he made a sweeping

148

motion with his hand. 'The house is no longer mine. I have no savings. But I leave you my deepest love. Go to my study and bring me *that book.*'

I knew at once which book he was referring to. I rose and made my way to the study, where I found thousands upon thousands of books stacked on shelves and piled on tables. I approached one of the shelves and selected *the book*.

I gave the book to my grandfather, and he rewarded me with a smile.

'Here is my legacy,' he said. 'Everything you need can be found within the covers of this book. Take it. Commit the book to memory.'

I took the book from my grandfather's trembling hand and I watched him die.

When I glanced at the cover, I saw I was holding a German copy of *Flight without End* by Joseph Roth. I opened the book and found an inscription, dedicated to my grandfather. It read, 'To Franz Tunda, my dearest friend—Fond Regards, Joseph.'

November 30, afternoon

I have spent the day pondering on grandpa's farewell gift. I have known for some time that grandpa named me after Roth. After all, Giuseppe is the Italian version of Joseph. But whenever I asked grandpa to tell me more about his friend, he would scurry away, as if hiding a precious stone from a greedy jeweller. Actually, it wasn't grandpa who first told me about Roth. I discovered him myself, by accident, about six years ago.

I had been visiting a sick friend in her home and we watched Ermanno Olmi's intriguing film *The Legend of the Holy Drinker*, based on Joseph Roth's novella of the same name. In that story a young down-and-out living in 1930s Paris is approached by a stranger who offers him two hundred francs on condition he repay the money to the priest who reads the mass at the Chapelle de Sainte Marie des Batignolles. The tramp squanders the money on wine, but is given repeated opportunities to redeem himself with new loans that turn up in miraculous ways. Sadly, I had to leave my friend before the concluding scene, where Andreas makes one final effort to repay the money. I phoned my friend the following morning to ask how the film had ended, but I learned to my consternation that she had fallen asleep during the film's climax.

When I told grandpa about the film he grew agitated and flapped his arms like a wounded sparrow.

'Never mind the film!' he shouted. 'Read the book!'

To be sure, I wanted to know how the story ended, but when I visited the *librerie* in Napoli, I discovered that the book was not available in Italian.

December 1

I awoke this morning with sharp hunger pangs and a dry mouth. I have been cooped up in the study for two days without food and water. I have been living in my thoughts since grandpa died and now my body is wreaking vengeance. I threw open the door of the study and stomped into the kitchen. I yanked the refrigerator open and pillaged it for food. I wolfed

150

down chunks of cheese and leftover salami. I found some stale bread in the cupboard and gulped down sour milk. To begin with, my heart was pounding and I felt dizzy.

Suddenly an eerie smell assaulted my nostrils. I made my cautious way to grandpa's bedroom—but I wish I hadn't. A foul stench was emanating from his body. His eyes, wide open, had begun to dissolve and his face seemed sunken. It was as if his body was in the process of caving in. I threw a blanket over the corpse and wondered whether to call the police. But after I'd regained my calm I saw the futility of contacting anyone. For a brief moment, I considered burying grandpa in the garden, among his beloved orchids. But that struck me as equally absurd. I even wondered whether I should set the house on fire.

Upon reflection, I packed a small suitcase with shirts, a razor and the *Flight without End*. I also threw in my passport, some blank notebooks and pencils—lots of pencils. I ransacked the house for such money as I could find. Then, just before I made my escape, I pocketed grandpa's gold watch.

I made my way to the Piazza Garibaldi. At the Stazione Centrale I bought a ticket to Roma. I boarded the express, but, as always, there was a last minute delay. I thought the train was never going to depart, when, all of a sudden I heard the shrill pierce of a whistle and the train gave a malicious jolt. The train moved along like an arthritic mastodon, lisping and spluttering. Then it picked up speed and I felt as if I were riding on the wings of a pterodactyl.

I remember now when I first read Roth. It was three years after the film and by then grandpa had taught me French and German.

I had been visiting Paris and there obtained a French translation of Roth's novella from a bookstore on the Boulevard Saint-Michel. No sooner had I paid for the book than I rushed to the nearest café, where I ordered a cognac and read the book from cover to cover in one sitting. I was shocked to discover that Andreas Kartak, the hero of the story, drinks himself to death. It was not entirely clear whether he had succeeded in repaying the money, but it was evident that he had genuinely tried.

What was it about Roth's story that charmed me? I think it was because Andreas repeatedly tells the reader that he is a man of honour; that he can be trusted to keep his word. What does it matter that he walks about in rags and stinks like a sewer? What does it matter that he first betrayed and later murdered his friend? Joseph Roth asks the reader to believe that no matter how much we harm ourselves and betray others there forever remains one last opportunity to redeem one's past.

The day after reading *Legend* I visited the American Library in Paris: I wanted to know more about Joseph Roth's life. I discovered, firstly, that Roth had pursued a career in journalism. He was a man of deep political convictions who voiced his views in his articles and in his fiction. Noticeably, Roth warned Europe about the dangers of Nazism; his first novel, *The Spider's Web*, was a biting indictment of Hitler's National Socialism. In 1920 Roth had moved to Berlin, where he worked as a journalist for the Frankfurter Zeitung from 1923 to 1932; and he continued his outspoken critique of the National Socialist party.

Then, one winter evening in 1933, as Joseph Roth sat in his apartment in Berlin, he realised that Hitler was destined to become Chancellor. He knew also that it would not take long before the Nazis sought revenge against him; and so he abandoned his apartment and took the early morning train to Paris.

I have often imagined that moment in Roth's life when—realising that his attempts to curb the rise of National Socialism had failed—he abandons Berlin, carrying the bare essentials: clean shirts, shaving implements and perhaps some small memento of the life he was leaving behind. In *The Legend of the Holy Drinker*, Andreas' possessions are carried in a small tin box: a passport (expired), some letters and a watch that his father had given to him.

It is night now and the train is pulling into Roma Termini. I will look for a hotel near the station. I feel tired, so tired, I could sleep forever. Tomorrow I will ponder my grandfather's request that I memorise *Flight*.

Roma, December 2

I have made an astounding discovery.

I awoke in a cramped shoe-box of a room in a *pensione* on the Via Castelfidardo. My first impulse upon awakening was to count the money I had brought with me from Napoli. I was immediately reassured: I had sufficient funds to last me five or six weeks, maybe more if I was frugal. Then I went to the breakfast room, where I ordered black coffee and nothing else. While the waitress was fetching my coffee I pulled *Flight* from out of my coat and I turned to the first page. I read: 'Franz Tunda, first lieutenant in the Austrian Army, became a Russian prisoner of war in August 1916.'

Suddenly the waitress returned with the coffee and I hid the book under the table. I must have looked guilty because the woman threw me a puzzled look before wandering off.

Blood was now throbbing in my brain. I pulled the book out from its hiding place and I flicked through the pages, stopping at a chapter here, perusing another chapter there. It didn't take me long to realise that I was holding a fragment of my grandfather's life. His struggles, his hopes, his loves—they were all recorded in this battered document—covering a ten-year period of his adventurous life—from Russia to France—from 1916 to 1926.

I gulped down my coffee and flew out onto the streets of the eternal city. Before long I found I had mounted the steps to the Corso Cavour. I stopped and stared at the deserted church of San Pietro in Vincoli. No, it was not the church that attracted my attention but a statue of Moses, sculpted by Michelangelo for Pope Julius II. Suddenly, I broke into a flood of tears. I was sobbing uncontrollably. My knees gave way and I flopped to the pavement at the foot of the statue.

Of all human emotions, grief is the most mysterious. In the midst of profound grief one feels that the end of the world is nigh, and that life no longer deserves to be lived. Then the tide turns and grief passes us by—and the beautiful things of this world light up once again. So it was that at length my tears dried up. I picked myself up from the ground and headed in the direction of the Tiber. I crossed the Ponte Fabricio and sat by the banks of the river on the Isola Tiberina.

And I began to read *Flight without End.*

I read how my grandfather escaped from his prison in Siberia and for three years he hid in the forest with a Polish hunter named Baranowicz. In 1919, when he hears that the war has ended he attempts to reach Vienna, but becomes embroiled in the Revolution. While fighting alongside the Red Army he meets Natasha Alexandrovna. But he soon becomes disillusioned with her ideals and so he flees to the Caucasus, where he takes up a secluded life with a half-Georgian woman, Alja. He marries Alja. He deserts her. He returns to Vienna, where he hopes to find his fiancée of long ago—Irene Hartmann—but she is married to another. My grandfather now flees to Germany, to a small city on the Rhine, and he stays with his brother George, an orchestra conductor. But grandpa discovers that George represents everything he hates about the new world. George is complacent and conformist, smug, empty and pretentious. So grandpa now flees to Berlin. Later he goes to Paris, where he hopes to meet up with Irene Hartman. But in Paris he encounters the same spiritual bankruptcy and at length the story ends with my grandfather standing alone on the Place de la Madeleine, aged thirty-two, lost, resigned, wondering where to go.

The novel ends: 'He had no occupation, no desire, no hope, and not even self-love. No one in the world was as superfluous as he.'

Roma, December 3

I have made up my mind to honour grandpa's last wish. I will memorise *Flight*.

Roma, December 9

For the last six days I have been struggling to memorise the book, but I have not got past the third page. I doubt that I will be capable of memorising the entire text. I am twenty-four years old and therefore at the peak of my intellectual abilities, but grandpa's task seems beyond me.

Roma, December 10

There is something else that has begun to preoccupy me.

I had been out all day, wandering in the Quirinale, feeling lost and homeless, when I happened to pass a shop that sells antiquities and I saw my reflection in a mirror. My face seemed horribly distorted: I looked pale and haggard and puffed up. I thought at first that it must have been an illusion created by the faint lights of the shop. But when I returned to the *pensione* and studied my countenance in the bedroom mirror, I re-alised that what I saw earlier was no trick of the light.

156

My dark hair has always been thick and parted down the side. But now my hair is thinning, and if I part it in my usual manner one can see a bald spot. My olive skin has turned ashen and my face is bloated. I even seem to have developed a slight stoop of the shoulders. It's obvious that recent events have aged me.

On the Train to Venezia, December 11
I lay awake in bed most of last night. Only when the first rays of dawn came to greet me through the thin and shabby curtains did I obtain some measure of sleep. I slept until eleven and when I opened my eyes I was besieged by the most frightening sense of nostalgia for the life I had left behind and an even more terrifying nausea for my present condition. Accordingly, I checked out of the hotel and hastily made my way to Roma Termini.

At the ticket office I asked the clerk to sell me a ticket, any ticket, to any destination. He looked aghast.

'The Signore wishes me to choose his destination?'

'That's right,' I said, 'you choose.'

'The express to Venezia is leaving in ten minutes. The Signore wishes to take this train?'

'The Signore wishes it, yes, yes—for God's sake just sell me the ticket!'—And that's how I came to be on this train.

Now that I am on the move again I feel a sense of relief. In a matter of hours I shall be in Venezia. But what will become of me? Where am I to go? Will I ever find happiness? Strange: it is only now that I have lost everything that I raise the question of happiness. Was my grandfather happy with his life? To be sure, grandpa did not live in this world. There was an aura of sadness about grandpa that I never could understand. He despised this world, it filled him with revulsion. The question of happiness never entered his mind: it was enough that he should endure.

My thoughts have been dwelling on grandpa's friend once again and the *Legend of the Holy Drinker*. Did Joseph Roth achieve a measure of happiness in his nomadic and turbulent life?

One of the surprising elements of Roth's enforced exile in France was how delighted and enamoured he became of France and the Mediterranean. Soon after arriving in Paris, Roth resumed his career as a journalist; he was commissioned to travel throughout France and beyond, and to report on what he saw.

When I visited the American Library in Paris I read Roth's journalistic pieces from the 1930s and it seemed to me that in his travels Roth experienced something akin to happiness. Certainly, he seemed to have found compensation for the loss of his original homeland, the Austro-Hungarian Empire. But when I glanced into the private world of Roth's letters, I became aware of another darker, more pessimistic vision of the world.

Shortly after his exile into France, Roth wrote to his friend Stefan Zweig, 'You will have realized by now that we are drifting towards great catastrophes. Apart from the private—our literary and financial existence is destroyed—it all leads to a new war. I won't bet a penny on our lives. They have succeeded in establishing a reign of barbarity. Do not fool yourself. Hell reigns.'

The Legend of the Holy Drinker tells the story of one man's desperate attempts to preserve his dignity in the face of a total collapse of his world. It should not surprise me, then, that underneath Roth's delight at finding a new home there lurked the nostalgia for an old world. Joseph Roth may have written enthusiastically about France and the world of the Mediterranean, but from 1933 until his death in 1939 he descended into alcoholism, poverty and homelessness.

Venezia, December 12

I have taken a luxurious room in the Centauro Hotel on Campo Manin. It is an expensive room, and perhaps it is more than I can afford. But Venezia is a magnificent city, beautiful beyond words—and it seems to hurl me into recklessness. In my imagination Venezia is also the city of death and decay. It was the setting for Thomas Mann's *Death in Venice* and that eerie film by Nicolas Roeg—*Don't Look Now*. A city of ghosts too— I'm thinking of *A Wicked Voice* by Vernon Lee and that strange novella by Robert Aickman, *Never Visit Venice*. Indeed, wherever I stroll I see beauty incomparable blending with the putrid smells of palaces growing mouldy with time. The sun glows nostalgically in the heavens, but the green-blue waters never light up.

I took the *motoscafo* to the Isola San Michele, reputed to be the most beautiful cemetery in Italy. And I was not disappointed. The island resembles a gigantic ship filled with graves and tall cypresses, domes and mausoleums. The cemetery delights me with its beauty as much as it intimidates me with its silence.

And there is a curious history to the island. In 1797 Napoleonic forces occupying Venezia gave the order that the citizens could no longer bury their dead in Venezia centre. A strange idea when one reflects upon it—can the living and the dead really be kept apart?

I chose a secluded corner of the island and I tried to memorise a passage from *Flight* by reading out loud, and then repeating what I had read. I had made considerable progress—I had memorised three pages—when, all at once I became aware of a Franciscan monk staring at me in wonder. I smiled at him to relieve my embarrassment, but he just continued to gaze at me until—at last—he pulled his hood over his head and with bent shoulders he scurried away like a frightened mouse.

Venezia, December 15

A curious incident took place this evening. Maybe I'm giving the event more attention than it deserves, but there is no denying that it has unsettled me.

After dusk I had gone out for a long wander through the winding narrow streets, and I had stopped at a small restaurant famous for its excellent *galani*. I had placed my order and was now perusing *Flight* when the waiter brought my wine. He asked me if the magazine belonged to me. Thinking that he was referring to my book, I indicated that I wished to read undisturbed. But when the waiter wandered off I realised that he had been referring to a magazine left behind by a previous customer. I read the title—it was a back issue of an Italian journal that specialized in strange true tales. Laying my Roth book to one side, I flicked through the pages of this unusual magazine, until my eyes alighted on an article that captured my imagination, entitled "A Chess Game with a Deceased Grandmaster." And I was midway through the article when the waiter brought my pasta, accompanied by a basket filled with crusty bread.

The article proved to be one of the most intriguing, if not exasperating, reports I had ever come across. I read that Viktor Korchnoi, grandmaster of chess and ten-times Candidate for the World Championship, had played a chess game with the deceased grandmaster, Géza Maróczy, over an eight year period, from 1985 to 1993. Maróczy was a Hungarian player who became the most successful grandmaster in the early years of the 20th century. Between 1899 and 1908 he competed in fifteen international tournaments and on every occasion won a top prize. In 1906 Géza Maróczy signed an agreement with Emmanuel Lasker—the reigning World Champion—to play a match for the World Title. But when the match failed to take place, Maróczy lost interest in chess and he played less often.

Géza Maróczy had been dead for thirty-four years when Korchnoi challenged him to a chess game. The match was arranged by Eisenbeiss, a keen amateur player. He approached Robert Rollans, a well-known medium (who had no knowledge of chess), and asked him if he could make contact with Maróczy. When asked to comment on his game with the deceased grandmaster, Korchnoi indicated that, to begin with, he had not been impressed by Maróczy's moves. The

Hungarian champion played in an old-fashioned manner and so Korchnoi quickly gained the advantage. But when the players reached the endgame Maróczy began to manoeuvre his pieces with greatest skill. Even so, Maróczy resigned the match after forty-eight moves.

When I left the restaurant and made my leisurely way to the hotel, I took the magazine with me, intending to read the strange article one more time. But my rational mind soon took possession of my thoughts. A ridiculous article, I thought. No doubt, the Korchnoi-Maróczy game was a hoax. The fact that the game was played over an eight-year period gave the organizers of this chess prank ample time in which to study the positions and work out the best moves for 'Maróczy'. Before I had reached the Centauro I had thrown the magazine away and laughed at my gullibility. But a troublesome thought kept nagging at my mind.

Why would Viktor Korchnoi, a respected grandmaster of the royal game and one of the greatest chess players of all time—why would he lend himself to such a hoax? I could only conclude that Korchnoi believed that he was truly playing against the deceased Maróczy. And what did he hope to achieve? If Korchnoi had wanted to learn Maróczy's chess technique he could have done so by studying the Hungarian's games.

It was gone midnight when I reached the hotel and asked for the key to my room. By now I regretted that I had neglected my Roth book all evening. I was disappointed, also, with the direction of my thoughts. I undressed with haste and sought to drown my mind's meanderings in the balm of sleep. Indeed, I soon fell asleep, but I was visited by an uncanny dream.

I dreamt that grandpa was at the foot of my bed, calling my name—except that my name was not Giuseppe. Then, to my horror, grandpa began to claw at my bedcovers. The covers fell off and I lay there naked, feeling vulnerable and overawed. Suddenly, I felt the touch of grandpa's icy index finger. I awoke in terror—and with a terrible craving for wine.

Venezia, December 17

I fear that my mind has become unbalanced. I have taken to drinking wine in the way others drink water. I get up in the morning and the first thing I do is to knock back alcohol. Coffee seems repugnant to me now. In fact, I need wine for just about any activity. I can't think straight unless I have a glass; I can't act on my thoughts unless I have another glass. Meanwhile, my physical deterioration matches my mental corrosion. I have gained weight. My face is as round as a football and my hair is scanty. I still have a few tufts around the side and an island of hair jutting out of my forehead. But my hands are bloated and my face is lined and white. Grandpa's death has aged me ten or fifteen years. I don't even feel young. At least if I felt energetic I would feel compensated for the loss of my youthful appearance, but I'm tired most of the time. I drag my feet around as if they were hauling a ball and chain.

One good thing has come out of the last few days: I have been memorising *Flight* with a certain measure of success. I have now memorised the first three chapters!

And I attribute my newfound accomplishments to the method that I devised. It was that ridiculous article on the Korchnoi—Maróczy match that inspired me. In the same way that a chess player will play through the games of a grandmaster and thus learn about chess technique, I too have learned about the hidden powers of human memory. The chess player who takes it upon himself to study the games of another player does so by reading the moves from a book and *moving the pieces with his fingers*. Thus, it struck me that chess knowledge is most likely stored in the fingertips. Up to now I have failed to memorise *Flight* using my limited intellectual abilities, so I am now memorising the book with my fingers.

I am copying the book out by hand, sentence by sentence, in pencil, and using the notebooks I have brought with me. As I copy the words onto paper I simultaneously read them out loud, conjuring in my imagination the colours and landscapes and human conflicts that they refer to. It's as if Roth himself were guiding my hand and teaching me everything he knows. Certainly, the more I copy, the more I learn about his unique way of seeing the world and his extraordinary command of the German language. How shall I describe it? It's as if I were taking a private lesson with the master—a master class with Joseph Roth.

Venezia, December 18

I had an unpleasant encounter with a stranger as I was sitting in a café on the Piazza di San Marco. I had become totally absorbed in copying out a section of *Flight* when a funny-looking man with a pointed beard sat at my table. He nodded to me once and lit a cigarette. I looked about the café, wondering why he couldn't sit further away, and soon the strange little man had pulled me into a discussion about books and how to write them. Obviously, he mistook me for a writer.

He told me he was from Milano and that he was retired. As a working man he had sold televisions, but now that he had time on his hands he was going to dedicate the remainder of his days to writing short stories. Then he gave a deep sigh and said that inspiration didn't come easy to him. So he had signed up on a writer's course and he'd been learning the craft.

'I realise now,' he said, caressing his beard, 'that if you're serious about the craft you just have to take a writing course.'

'What makes you say that?' I said, making an effort to appear polite.

'These writing instructors, they teach you the dos and don'ts. Grab your reader from the first line. Don't use adjectives. Write what you know. Find your voice.—I couldn't have worked these formulas out on my own.'

'But—in the past—how did writers learn their craft?'

'What do you mean?'

'I mean that writers like Dante and Dickens and Goethe and Pushkin—they didn't attend writing courses. They just wrote and learned from experience.'

'I see what you're getting at,' he said, with a dismissive wave of his hand, 'but it's obvious: they must have had private lessons.'

'Who with?'

'Why, with other writers, older and more experienced.'

'And these older, more experienced writers—where did they learn to write?'

My companion gave me an appraising look, tugged at his beard—and said he had to leave. He leapt to his feet, mumbled a farewell and scampered away. To be sure, our conversation hadn't lasted long, but the stranger left me in an irritable state of mind, and I could not concentrate for the rest of the afternoon.

Venezia, later the same evening

Following today's bizarre conversation with the short story writer, I have decided to stay in my hotel until I have completed my project of memorising *Flight*.

On a train, December 28

I have had to leave Venezia and I am writing these lines on a train. But I have no idea where the train is heading to—and I have not been able to locate the guard for information. Indeed, I have marched up and down the length of the train and it appears that I am the only passenger.

It happened like this.

I had been keeping to my hotel room, memorising *Flight*, and barely going out except to eat and obtain more wine. I had given up on sleep. I had become so absorbed in my project that the world had ceased to exist for me. Then, yesterday afternoon I copied the last chapter of Roth's book. When I tried to recite one of the chapters I found that I could do so only imperfectly. I thought that I had failed and I was enveloped by a mist of despondency. Suddenly, it occurred to me to write the chapter out and I was thrilled to discover that I could write out any chapter to perfection.

I jumped for joy and stomped about in my hotel room, dancing like a monkey. I made such a racket that I expected my neighbours to pound on the walls—but my excitement was met by silence. Then I washed and shaved and changed into a clean outfit. I was looking forward to a hearty evening meal in a restaurant and a bottle of Chianti.

As I made my exit I noticed that there was no one at the reception desk. I stopped and looked about. I wondered that the reception area was entirely bereft of activity. Then I shrugged my shoulders and stepped out into the Venetian night. No sooner had I found myself outside than I was assailed by a spiteful wind and an uncanny winter chill. I plunged my hands into my coat pockets, I hunched my shoulders, and I walked along the deserted streets, keeping my eyes on the ground.

Then—I came to a sudden halt.

Venezia is a city that never sleeps. The city centre is always buzzing and droning with human voices and the sound of footsteps. But as I stood there in the halflight of a narrow lane, I could feel the silence pressing on my body.

I hurried along, making my way towards the city centre. I felt the icy touch of dread and—like Edgar Allan Poe's man of the crowd—I longed for human contact.

I looked up at the clear sky and saw a beautiful malignant moon casting its silvery flakes of light. I quickened my steps. I broke into a run. At last I came out onto the Piazza di San Marco—the vibrant centre that never rests—and I halted in the very centre of the square.

The Piazza was deserted.

I stood there and looked about me, my eyes craving for some sign of life. By now I had fallen into a strange calmness mingled with profound fear. I hurried along past the Biblioteca Nazionale and came out onto the Riva dei Schiavoni. The gondolas were floating gently on water, but there was no one to man them. I now raced along the Riva and passed over the Ponte della Paglia, turning my gaze in every direction. In the distance I heard church bells tolling the eleventh hour. I retraced my steps and headed in a north westerly direction; but long before I reached the Rialto I knew that I was alone in a dead city.

I returned to the hotel. I packed my suitcase and fled the Centauro.

Shortly before midnight, I reached Venezia Santa Lucia and I walked up to the ticket office, but there was no one at the window. No one in the station—no guards—no tourists—no one to guide me out of the nightmare. I wandered about the station with dejected steps, resigned to the Unknown. Then—as I glanced at the station platforms I saw a train getting ready to leave. Where was it going? But I wasn't granted time to check its destination, for I heard the whistle that signals a departure and the train began to heave its mammoth weight out of the station.

I ran towards that train as if it were my only hope. I had dashed out onto the platform, and I thought that I would never get on board—for the train had picked up speed. I threw myself into a desperate burst of energy. I ran and caught up with the last carriage—I flung open the door—I threw my suitcase in—and I heaved myself up onto the train.

My lungs were exploding. I had to lean against the wall and catch my breath. At last I recovered control of my body and I began the search for a guard or a fellow passenger. I darted from carriage to carriage, from the rear of the train to the front. But the train was as empty of souls as the city I had left behind.

Many Hours Later

I know now where I am, and where I am going. More importantly, I understand the transformations I have been going through. The loss of hair, the rapid ageing, the unquenchable thirst for wine—these are the inevitable indicators of a more profound change.

When I realised that I was the sole passenger of this ghost train, I chose a compartment and waited for my destiny. As the train shot through the liquid blackness of night, I fell into a deep and dreamless sleep with my head resting on my suitcase. When I awoke, I saw fingers of sunlight gripping the horizon. I looked out the window and was mesmerised by the passing telegraph wires, like so many giants rushing past me with a whoosh. My eyes drank in the barren landscape. Then I heard the patter of raindrops against the side of the train and my window became blurred by the rolling drops upon the glass.

Suddenly I heard clanging and scraping—a door opened and closed—footsteps—followed by silence. Then—the door to my compartment was torn open—and I saw two men standing at the entrance, staring.

After a pause, they entered.

I looked up and studied their faces. They were both men in their prime, but on their lips and in their eyes I could detect a cruelty that took my breath away. The taller of the two men was dressed in a dark suit. His companion stood with his hands in the pockets of a grimy grey-green raincoat.

It was the tall man who addressed me.

'Bitte, mein Herr—your passport.'

'Who are you?' I said, addressing my question to the tall man.

'We are police officers. We'd like to see your papers.'

'Where is the guard? No one has asked me for my ticket.'

'That is no concern of ours—or yours,' said the man in the raincoat.

A long pause followed. But I could feel the hostility of the men mounting with every passing second. I fetched my suitcase and pulled out my old and battered passport. The tall man snatched the document with a sneer. He flicked through its pages without sign of interest. I glanced over at his companion, but I could not read his face. At length the tall man spoke.

'You will state your name, your occupation and your place and date of birth.'

'It's all in that document that you are holding,' I said, irritably.

The man in the raincoat stepped closer to me and said, 'All the same, we'd like to hear it from you.'

An extraordinary event now followed. It was as if all my life I had been waiting for this moment, for the opportunity to state my name. From the depths of my being, an image arose—it was the vision of a blanket being laid over my grandfather's dead body by a young Giuseppe. And in that instant I knew that I was Giuseppe no longer.

I looked up at the police officers and in a voice laced with calm, I said, 'My name is Joseph Roth. I was born on the second of September 1894 in the town of Brody in Galicia. My father's name is Nochum, my mother's is Mirjam. I live in Berlin on the Potsdamer Strasse, and I work as a journalist for the Franfurter Zeitung. And so, gentlemen, you now know who I am. And if you have no further questions, I'd like to have my passport back.'

A silence followed, but it was brief—and the tall man returned my passport.

Two hours later

My first impulse, when the train pulled into Berlin Südkreuz, was to rush to the nearest newsagent and glance at the top corner of the Neue Berliner Zeitung.

Today is January 29—and the year is 1933.

To know one's destiny, to know one's place in the grand scheme called history, brings with it a strange feeling akin to anxiety, only deeper and more disturbing.

I spent the morning wandering the snow-laden streets of Berlin, fighting against the impulse to go to the Frankfurter Zeitung. I wanted to see my colleagues. I longed to return to a regular routine, perhaps to pretend that all was well with the world and that I could continue my life as a journalist in Berlin with all the privileges that I had acquired over the years. But I knew that I had only hours to play with: I would be leaving Berlin in the early hours of the following morning. And so—

I made my way to Mampe's Gute Stube, my favourite café-restaurant located on the Kurfürstendamm— and there I sat drinking wine and conversing with the locals, harvesting the gossip of the day. I had long since learned the power of the anecdote, and as a journalist I would plunder the local bars and bistros for a juicy tale. I first learned the subversive quality of the anecdote when I read Herodotus' *Histories*. As a young man I could not grasp why in heavens Herodotus sprinkled his historical records with local gossip. But later, when I had read Suetonius' *Lives of the Caesars* and Procopius' *Secret History*, I came to understand the supremacy of the anecdote and the rebellious nature of the oral tale.

It was late afternoon when I left Mampe's. I had had a good many glasses of red wine, and little in the way of food. But I had put together the pieces of

172

Berlin's political puzzle. Two months previously, the National Socialist party had failed to gain a majority of votes in the Reichstag. Indeed, Hitler's popularity had dwindled, and it was rumoured that Hitler had considered suicide. But Franz von Papen, the present Chancellor, had been unable to gain sufficient support in the Reichstag. It was said that Paul Hindenburg and von Papen were governing Germany on a shoe-string of power and that together they had approached Hitler and offered him the position of Vice-Chancellor. Hitler had refused: he demanded to be made Chancellor. And von Papen and Hindenburg were weighing up the risks.

I hurried along the heaving streets of Berlin and made my way to the small hotel on the Potsdamer Strasse that been my last refuge in Germany. En route I bought a bottle of red wine and a loaf of bread. On reaching the hotel, I was bid a hearty welcome by the concierge. I gave him a hasty *Grüss Gott*, taking care not to stop and chatter. I mounted the steps to the first floor and stood before the door to my apartment. Where was the key? I searched my pockets and my suitcase without success. I was on the verge of asking the concierge for help when, suddenly, I turned and faced the door. Whether I was guided by instinct or memory, I do not know, but my fingers searched the top rim of the door and there I found the key.

I entered.

It was a small room, made smaller by the clutter of excess furniture. A table and two chairs stood by a solitary window. Leaving my suitcase in the middle of the room, I placed the wine on the table and stepped into the kitchen. A moment later I returned with two glasses of wine and a corkscrew. I uncorked the wine. Remembering suddenly that I had stashed the loaf of bread in my coat pocket, I placed this morsel of food on the table and sat and waited.

Outside my window a mantle of darkness had spread across the city. I could hear the wind's icy fingers tapping on the panes of the glass. And every now and then I heard a voice from the streets, like a lonely hermit saying his prayers for the night. But the hotel was silent, my room was silent, the stairs and the landing were silent—and the minutes ticked into hours—heavy, sad, painful hours of waiting. Every now and then my fingers pinched the loaf and I would swallow a crumb without delight. But I didn't touch the wine.

Shortly before midnight, I heard a door bang on the ground floor. There were footsteps—slow, methodical steps making their way to the first floor. They dragged along the landing and came to a halt outside my apartment. I waited for the knock, but the visitor did not announce his presence. I saw the handle of the door turn softly. The hinges gave their shrill alarm. I saw a hand—a head—and the visitor stepped into my home.

'Hello Joseph,' he said, casting his eyes on the wine, 'I see you haven't changed your ways.'

I looked up at the visitor's countenance and recognized my old friend Franz Tunda. He was standing by the door in a dark leather jacket and in battered worker's boots.

I leapt to my feet. We embraced. Then we sat at the table and I poured the wine. I knocked back my glass while Franz sipped his wine as if he were nibbling a piece of cheese. And we gazed at each other for a stretch of time until at length I could stand the silence no longer.

'When did you quit Paris?' I said.

'I've been in Berlin for a week now. As soon as I arrived I went to the Frankfurter Zeitung and asked after you. Some said you were in the south of France; others that you were in Munich on a special assignment. I realised at once that they didn't have a clue. I came here also—several times—and banged on your door. Say, Joseph—do you have a cigarette?'

I shook my head no.

'Shame,' said Franz, with a shrug of a shoulder.

'But what are you doing in Berlin?' I asked.

'I don't really know. Maybe I've come to see you. Maybe I'm on my way...'

'...to a better place?' I said—and we both burst into laughter.

Franz crossed his arms and leaned his elbows on the table.

'I'm old enough to know that there is no such place. One government is as vile and fraudulent as another. You know, Joseph, it's in our nature: we create laws to protect each other. But humans are pitiful creatures— flawed in the very centre of their being—and so our laws are flawed too. No, we will never be able to create a better place.'

'Where, then, do you intend to go?'

'Italy. I will go south to Rome or Naples. But don't get me wrong: I'm not expecting to find a safe haven. I just need to go somewhere.—And what about you? What will become of you?'

'I'm leaving for Paris—tonight.'

'And what in the heavens,' exclaimed Franz, 'do you intend to do there?'

'If I'm lucky, I'll live in a hotel. If not, I'll sleep under the Pont Neuf. Either way I shall drink myself to death.'

'I never liked your jokes, Joseph—I like them even less now.'

'Listen to me Franz,' I said, refilling our glasses, 'if you follow my instructions we will meet again. Did I ever tell you why I became a journalist? No? Well, it's simple: I took to writing for the newspapers because I despaired of doing any other profession. Writing was my only skill. But I was deceived about my talent. I thought I could wield my pen and change the human condition. But I didn't understand my place in history—I didn't understand my fellow human beings—I didn't realise the power and folly of language.'

'I suppose you know better now?'

'Please, Franz, don't interrupt. We don't have a lot of time. Tonight or tomorrow morning Hitler will be made Chancellor. By midday of January 30 the entire nation will know that the course of history has been changed. Many will rejoice at what they believe is the rejuvenation of the German people. Others will suffer death or exile. You see, history is not just something that we do: it is also something that is done to us.'

I studied my friend's face and saw that my words had fallen on deaf ears. I reached into the inner pocket of my coat and I pulled out *Flight without End.*

I placed the book between us.

'See this?'

'It's your book,' Franz said, 'you wrote it.'

'Yes and no. Listen. A few days ago, in Venice, I met a strange little man who thought one can learn to write in the way one learns to brush one's teeth. Oh, I dare say one can teach grammar; one can teach a person how to construct a good sentence. But literature cannot be taught any more than history. You have to have a feeling for literature—a deep unfaltering love for its infinite gifts.'

Silence fell upon us. Franz reached for the book. With his index finger he pulled back the cover and read the inscription with my signature.

'I wrote this book,' I went on, 'but at the time that I copied the book I was not yet the author. You look surprised. Yes, that's right! I copied the book out by hand, in pencil, word for word. I memorised this book until I became at one with the author. And in that silent communion with the author of this painful tale, I came to see the true shape of history. At last I understood my fellow human beings. I remembered who I was—and I saw the tragedy of Hitler's Germany unfold before my eyes.'

Another pause followed. I could read confusion in Franz's eyes. I leaned forwards, and, in a hoarse whisper, I made a final effort.

'Franz, this book is not just a collection of words. It's not even a message for those who have the time to read it. It is a testament to our friendship. It is my gift to you. Take it. Keep it close to you. And in the years to come, be sure to hand this book to a loved one.'

Franz looked at me, amazed. 'Who shall I give it to?'

'Give it to your grandson. If you do, I promise you, Franz, I will find my way back to you. I will cross the chasm of time and we will sit here once again, talking and drinking, in defiance of the dark night of history.'

Presently, Franz grasped the book with both hands. I poured out the dregs of the wine. Somewhere in the vast German night a bell tolled the first hour of the morning.

Berlin, January 30, 1933, in the early hours of the morning

Franz and I arrived at the Lehrter Bahnhof shortly before sunrise and we waited for the west-bound train. The air was stabbing us with its icy needles. Every now and then Franz would flap his arms and stomp about in a desperate effort to keep warm.

'Joseph—are you sure you don't have a cigarette?'

'Be patient, Franz. I promise you: in Italy you will never go cold.'

'To hell with patience! I'd give anything for a good piece of tobacco.'

The train arrived puffing and fuming. It stopped with a loud screech—like the cry of an owl in pain. And soon the stationmaster was blowing the whistle for all aboard. I staggered into a compartment at the rear end of the train and found an unoccupied seat by the window. I threw my suitcase onto the luggage rack. Then I climbed down from the train and gave Franz a final embrace. I tried to find a suitable phrase with which to say goodbye, but Franz kept looking at his boots. At length the whistle blew and I boarded the train as it heaved and slithered its way along the tracks. I saw then that Franz was running alongside my window, waving his arms and calling my name.

I pulled down the glass and asked if there was something the matter.

'Joseph! When you get to Paris, be sure to ask for *cigarettes sans filtre.*'

Franz could no longer keep up with the train. I leaned out and gazed at my friend until he was no more than a shivering black dot in the distance. At last I stumbled into my seat and I gave a crazy tearful laugh.

Yes Franz, when I reach Paris I will add smoking to my list of vices.

ABOUT THE STORIES

THE STORIES collected in this volume represent nine different experiments in writing. To be sure, all of the stories feature the supernatural or the long arm of coincidence. But despite my love of the strange and macabre, I do not regard these stories as traditional supernatural tales. The fantastic element in these stories merely represents their 'syntax' or 'grammar.' My purpose was to raise questions about the clash between human desire and history; between friendship and the temptation to betrayal; between the longing for the infinite and the certainty of death.

I wrote *Night Sea Journey to Turku* while relaxing on a beach in Sri Lanka in January 2005. I had always wanted to write a story in which some brief incident in the protagonist's youth turns out to be more important than an entire lifetime of mundane achievements, but such an idea is not easily carried out. Indeed, I believe that the only writer to have achieved such an effect is the Russian, Ivan Bunin. Some readers have wondered whether the woman on the ship is a ghost; or whether the 'lovers' made love. I think these questions miss the most beautiful moment of the story, which is when the sun shines in the woman's hair. From that moment onwards, the young man's life becomes a form of death. And it is only on the day he dies that he lives again. The reference to Homer's verses tells the reader that the structure to this story is the simplest and most ancient of all narrative formats: the journey. And my refusal to give names to the characters is entirely consistent with the mythic roots of this tale. I entered this story in the national short story competition sponsored by Dark Tales magazine in the autumn of 2008. Three months later I discovered that it had won third prize. The story was published in volume XIII of Dark Tales in March 2009 and dedicated to William Heinesen, in fond memory of an afternoon spent in Copenhagen in the autumn of 1983.

Into the Atacama 1899 was originally entitled *Girl with the Hollow Eyes*. But as there is a famous story by Fritz Leiber called *Girl with the Hungry Eyes*, a change of title was deemed necessary. My story is set in Chile at the end of the nineteenth century. Valparaiso, the city from which Don Francisco flees, is portrayed as the epitome of human corruption. The desert to which he retires—the Atacama—is indeed the loneliest and driest place on earth. And because it has no human use, it takes on a spiritual quality that lures the protagonist into the wilderness in the form of a girl without eyes. This is a story of supernatural love in the tradition of Leo Perutz's *By Night under a Stone Bridge* or Alexander Lernet-Holenia's *Baron Bagge*. More importantly, I believe, it is a mystical tale that subverts materialism by presenting it as a form of death-in-life. In writing this story I have drawn on my reading of *Dark Night of the Soul* by Saint John of the Cross; as well as my memory of one of the most astonishing supernatural love stories I have ever read: *Twenty Years a Dream* by Pu Songling (1640—1715). Pu Songling's compilation of hundreds of stories and sketches represents one of the finest achievements in world literature, and one of the most outstanding collections of weird fiction.

The Devil Only Visits is a strange tale, and the reader is asked to approach this story in the same spirit he or she would read a story by Daniil Kharms or Ambrose Bierce. A young priest travelling to Valparaiso (circa 1900) listens to a tall tale told by an elegant elderly man who may or may not be the Devil. Now, I have always wondered what such an encounter might be like, and in my imagination I picture the Devil spinning an extraordinary tale which is historically, theologically, philosophically and psychologically implausible. Thus, in my story, the old man's theological argument that our sins preserve us from evil is outrageous; Lobito's reasons for seeking an encounter with Lucifer are psychologically far-fetched; and Don Lucca's stated intention of educating the priest's soul is laughable. Should the reader be offended by the image of the crabs digging their pincers into Christ, I would remind him or her that this shocking image is precisely the kind of nonsense that the Devil would conjure up—assuming, of course, that one believes in such a being. And here I might reveal a curious true incident.

While visiting Santiago de Chile in 1993 I was approached by a priest who asked me, 'How's your faith these days?' When I replied that I wasn't sure, he put both his hands on my head and muttered an extraordinary prayer. Later that evening, I had a terrifying dream in which I saw the Devil climbing into my room through the window. I tried to scream but my tongue was paralyzed. Then, I felt the Devil's fists pounding my legs. At last, I awoke and switched on the light—and when I tried to move my legs I found that they were sore. Days later, my brother Fernando and I took the bus from Santiago to Valparaiso; and I asked him if he believed in the Devil. He startled me by saying that, as a historian, he was forced to believe and that 'Lucifer's activities had been well documented for centuries.' All these strange incidents eventually found their way into my crazy story.

In the spring of 2007 my university granted me an academic sabbatical to go work abroad. To begin with I visited Saint Petersburg University and later, in the summer of that year, I made research contacts at the Institute for Human Sciences in Vienna. It was during my stay in Vienna that I conceived *Colonel Redl's Knife Sheath*, a spy story set in 1913. This story required considerable historical research, and I am pleased to say that the names and dates and major events reported are authentic. The protagonist of this story, Detective Sergeant Ebinger, is based on the intelligence officer of that name who did indeed discover that Colonel Alfred Redl was in the employ of Russian Intelligence. Of course, the dialogue is fictitious, as is the final meeting between Redl and Ebinger. But the real interest of this story is the tension between the historical events that are recounted by Ebinger and the unreliable quality of his narration. Ebinger's guilt is out of all proportion with his faults. Moreover, he exaggerates his involvement in the downfall of the Monarchy. He neither understands his own emotions, nor the emotions of others. In many respects, he reminds me of that other famous unreliable narrator—Lermontov's Pechorin. The net result is that Ebinger does not understand his place in history (emphasized by Redl's reference to Herodotus), and this makes this story a philosophical reflection on chance and historicity. Upon re-reading this story I detected the influence of the anonymous author of *Njal's Saga*, and also, of that eccentric French film-maker, Jean-Pierre Melville.

When I was twelve years old and living in Santiago de Chile, I attended a Catholic school named Saint George's College. The school was run by American priests and nuns, and situated on the Avenida Pedro de Valdivia. One day, we were taken to the school chapel for a mass. The fact that the mass was on a Wednesday afternoon was in itself unusual, but I also remember that as the priest delivered his sermon a strange sound emanated from the boy sitting next to me. Suddenly, the boy fell to the ground with arms thrashing—the priest commanded us to leave the chapel—and as I fled the chapel I looked back and saw the priest forcing his fingers down the boy's throat. I can still recall the feeling of absolute terror that this incident instilled in me, for this was my first intimation of death. Twenty-five years later, I attended a party in north London where a lovely flirtatious skinny woman invited me to spend the night at her home. That night I awoke and witnessed my companion trembling violently. These two epileptic attacks, although separated by a quarter of a century and in different parts of the world, became linked in my memory. To be precise, somewhere in the darker regions of my mind there lay the equation: mystical longings = death = lust.

It was to exorcise this bizarre conjunction of ideas that I wrote *The Possessed* on a lazy spring afternoon in 2009. I wrote the entire story in one sitting with only minimal corrections afterwards. But I had been mulling over the raw material of the story for many years. The entire narrative is constructed on a series of metonymic surprises whereby Harry, the protagonist, loses track of what he's really searching for. Hopefully, the reader will lose himself in the oedipal displacements that lead our hero from one futile desire to another, until we arrive at the last scene in which Harry, now a grown man, encounters the three elements of this spiritual equation. There are two symbolic codes that add depth to the narrative. One is the story (within a story) of the exorcisms of the legendary Père Surin. The other is the reference to *Vera*, a supernatural tale by Villiers de L'Isle Adam; a magnificent story about the power of love over death. Although the title of my story is not particularly original, I was reluctant to choose another: the present title links my story to the film of the same name by Ken Russell.

Orkney Crossing is an autobiographical short story. Set in Scotland in 1979, it describes how I narrowly missed injury or perhaps even death thanks to a premonitory dream. In October of that year, I was studying for my Bachelors degree in psychology at Brunel University. It was my final year and I was bitterly disappointed with theoretical psychology—a disappointment which has dogged me throughout my professional career. It was indeed 'to do something wild' before graduating that I fled to Edinburgh with my good friend Arturo. The dream that I had on October 21—22, 1979, was possibly the most terrifying nightmare that I have ever experienced, but it may have saved my life. If I had not remembered the dream at Edinburgh train station on the morning of October 22, I would have boarded the Aberdeen Express which crashed at Invergowrie later that day. Instead, I took a different train, and when I reached Thurso on the afternoon of October 22 and discovered that I had escaped the crash, I carried out an experiment which I had dreamed about as an adolescent: I disappeared. Of course, my actions were morally reprehensible and caused heartache to friends and family. But who has not dreamed of going missing, if only for a brief fragment of time? Over the years I have come to believe that the need for anonymity can be as powerful as the need for intimacy. In my story, the tension between these needs is expressed through the fictional character of Carol. How else are we to make sense of her wish to share her childhood refuge with me, only to abandon me 'at the back of the north wind?' I wrote this story using Jack Kerouac's method of spontaneous prose and after the first draft I made only one revision.

Meyrink's Gambit is a story about an impossible chess game. Perhaps I should mention that chess has played an important role in my life. As a child I used to visit my grandfather on Saturday afternoons and we would immerse ourselves for hours in games of chess and in analyses of grandmaster chess positions. These silent communions with my grandfather represent some of the happiest memories of my childhood. After my grandfather's death I neglected chess and only returned to the game after a lapse of sixteen years. I composed chess studies that were published in Europe and North America. Then I took to playing correspondence chess with opponents from all over the world. I reached the master class in correspondence chess after winning two candidates tournaments. But when computers began to dominate the game I lost interest in the 'game of kings.'

In *Meyrink's Gambit* I have combined my love of chess with my fascination with two personages from the early twentieth century: the visionary Gustav Meyrink and the artist Alfred Kubin. The premise of the story is rather fantastic: Meyrink predicts the fall of the Habsburgs after losing a chess game to Alfred Kubin. It's not known precisely when and where Kubin and Meyrink met. Mike Mitchell, in his biography of Meyrink, speculates it may have been around 1907, although the two men had certainly corresponded from 1904 onwards. In my story, Kubin and Meyrink meet in 1913, in the Café Museum. Sadly, this coffee house closed down in the 1990s and was replaced by an ice-cream parlour. To return to the story—besides the mysterious workings of chance, the story depicts a subtle use of the supernatural. To be sure, there is not much of a plot, but my aim in this story has been, above all, to evoke the lost world of early twentieth century Vienna.

Doña Ariana's Glass Foot is a strange tale in the tradition of Pu Songling, and influenced by that master of the minimalist short story, Daniil Kharms. The story is set in a mythical San Francisco and it may be that when I conceived this story I was inadvertently influenced by my obsessive love for Alfred Hitchcock's *Vertigo*. A young archaeology student is driven to love an older woman because he has accidentally stepped on her foot. The youth's guilt is out of all proportion to his misdeed. On the other hand, when he strangles the old woman he appears calm and resigned to fate. The youth's name—Vincent—is a touch of irony. The name derives from the Latin for 'he who vanquishes', but the character is far from being a heroic figure. The lady's name—Ariana—is derived from the Latin for spider. The final conversation between Bianca and Vincent has echoes of Aeschylus' *Oedipus Rex*. As for the repeated allusions to 'a certain lady'—that's just the writer poking fun at the reader.

A Master Class with Joseph Roth, the last story in this collection, is also its centrepiece. On the death of his grandfather, a young man defies time and the Nazis so as to share a glass of wine with a friend. This simple plot expresses everything I hold dear about friendship, literature and history. I wrote this story as a tribute to my literary master and mentor, Joseph Roth (even though this story also shows the influence of the intimate diaries of Arthur Schnitzler and the Lady Sarashina). The world of Joseph Roth's stories, novellas and novels is a realm that I have lived in ever since I read my first Roth book, *The Legend of the Holy Drinker*. And in the summer of 2005 I carried out one of the strangest literary experiments. Over a period of four months, from May to August of that year, I copied Roth's novel *The Radetzky March* by hand, using pencil and paper. I did this as a tribute to the writer of that wonderful novel. I was in Vienna when I copied out the last sentence of that book. It was about eleven o'clock in the evening and I was sitting on a bench on a lonely square, illuminated by a solitary dim street lamp. A policeman approached me and asked what I was doing. I showed him my notebook, but all I could think to say was, 'It is done!'

This story is also a tribute to that wonderful storyteller, my grandfather, Jorge Berguño Meneses. In many ways, the world of *The Radetzky March* represents the world of my grandfather, who was a soldier, playwright and chess player. When I had completed my task of copying Roth's book, I realised—to my intense astonishment—that all my scribbling was an attempt to reach my grandfather's world; a world that I associate with honour and loyalty. I realised also—to my profound sadness—how much I wanted to be granted one last afternoon with him. It is therefore fitting that the protagonist of my story, the young

190

Giuseppe, should defy time and Hitler in order to share a last glass of wine with a friend who, in another realm, is also his grandfather.

I would like to end these notes with grateful acknowledgements to friends who gave their support to this, my first, collection of short stories. First and foremost, I want to thank my friend, Lesley Millane, for patiently commenting on the first drafts of all the stories. I have learned a lot about writing by listening to her emotional reactions to my use of language and twists of plot. I would also like to convey my profound gratitude to the poet James Greene for reading the entire manuscript and pointing out my bizarre quirks of grammar. More importantly, James has been encouraging me for years to find a publisher and urged me never to give up. Special thanks go to Will Brooker of Kingston University, who provided me with critical comments to most of the stories; and to my brother Fernando Berguño, who introduced me to Alexander Lernet-Holenia. I would also like to mention my friend and colleague, Michael Staudigl of the Institute for Human Sciences in Vienna, for lending me material on Colonel Alfred Redl. Finally, I would like to express my deepest gratitude to my first publisher, Dan Ghetu, for sharing my literary obsessions.

A PARTIAL LIST OF SNUGGLY BOOKS

G. ALBERT AURIER *Elsewhere and Other Stories*
CHARLES BARBARA *My Lunatic Asylum*
S. HEZOLNRY BERTHOUD *Misanthropic Tales*
LÉON BLOY *The Tarantulas' Parlor and Other Unkind Tales*
ÉLÉMIR BOURGES *The Twilight of the Gods*
CYRIEL BUYSSE *The Aunts*
JAMES CHAMPAGNE *Harlem Smoke*
FÉLICIEN CHAMPSAUR *The Latin Orgy*
BRENDAN CONNELL *Metrophilias*
BRENDAN CONNELL *Spells*
BRENDAN CONNELL (editor)
    The World in Violet: An Anthology of EnglishDecadent Poetry
RAFAELA CONTRERAS *The Turquoise Ring and Other Stories*
DANIEL CORRICK (editor)
    Ghosts and Robbers: An Anthology of German Gothic Fiction
ADOLFO COUVE *When I Think of My Missing Head*
QUENTIN S. CRISP *Aiaigasa*
LUCIE DELARUE-MARDRUS *The Last Siren and Other Stories*
LADY DILKE *The Outcast Spirit and Other Stories*
CATHERINE DOUSTEYSSIER-KHOZE *The Beauty of the Death Cap*
ÉDOUARD DUJARDIN *Hauntings*
BERIT ELLINGSEN *Now We Can See the Moon*
ERCKMANN-CHATRIAN *A Malediction*
ALPHONSE ESQUIROS *The Enchanted Castle*
ENRIQUE GÓMEZ CARRILLO *Sentimental Stories*
DELPHI FABRICE *Flowers of Ether*
DELPHI FABRICE *The Red Sorcerer*
DELPHI FABRICE *The Red Spider*
BENJAMIN GASTINEAU *The Reign of Satan*
EDMOND AND JULES DE GONCOURT *Manette Salomon*
REMY DE GOURMONT *From a Faraway Land*
REMY DE GOURMONT *Morose Vignettes*
GUIDO GOZZANO *Alcina and Other Stories*
GUSTAVE GUICHES *The Modesty of Sodom*
EDWARD HERON-ALLEN *The Complete Shorter Fiction*
EDWARD HERON-ALLEN *Three Ghost-Written Novels*
J.-K. HUYSMANS *The Crowds of Lourdes*
J.-K. HUYSMANS *Knapsacks*
COLIN INSOLE *Valerie and Other Stories*
JUSTIN ISIS *Pleasant Tales II*